2006 上海工业发展报告

SHANGHAI INDUSTRIAL DEVELOPMENT REPORT

上海市经济委员会

SHANGHAI ECONOMIC COMMISSION

上 海 科 学 技 术 文 献 出 版 社

SHANGHAI SCIENTIFIC AND TECHNOLOGICAL LITERATURE PUBLISHING HOUSE

图书在版编目（CIP）数据

2006上海工业发展报告/上海市经济委员会
—上海：上海科学技术文献出版社，2006.6
ISBN 7-5439-2952-X

Ⅰ.2... Ⅱ.上... Ⅲ.工业经济－经济发展－研究
报告－上海市－2006 Ⅳ.F427.51

中国版本图书馆CIP数据核字（2006）第047069号

责任编辑：忻静芬

2006上海工业发展报告

上海市经济委员会

＊

上海科学技术文献出版社出版发行

（上海市武康路2号 邮政编码200031）

全 国 新 华 书 店 经 销

上海市北书刊印刷有限公司印刷

＊

开本889×1194 1/16 印张7.5 字数201 000

2006年6月第1版 2006年6月第1次印刷

印数：1-1700

ISBN 7-5439-2952-X/Z·1091

定价：30.00元

http://www.sstlp.com

编委会成员

前 言

"十五"期间，上海工业抓住新一轮国际产业转移和我国工业化、城市化发展的历史机遇，认真落实科学发展观和科教兴市主战略，坚持走新型工业化道路，强化创新、提升能级、发展装备、建设基地，继续保持了快速、协调、平稳的发展态势，较好地完成了"十五"各项经济指标，连续16年保持两位数增长。

《2006上海工业发展报告》（以下简称《报告》）全面回顾了"十五"期间上海工业的发展历程以及2005年上海工业的发展状况，以产业的技术创新为主线，全面反映了上海工业重点行业发展的基本情况，分析了2006年上海工业发展面临的机遇和挑战，提出了2006年发展的若干重点工作。《报告》体现如下特点：

1. 重点反映了上海工业的主要发展历程和趋势

《报告》通过对全市工业和主要产业经济运行状况的概述与分析，客观地反映了上海工业"十五"期间和2005年在"发展中调整"，实施战略性调整重组，优化产业发展布局，推进工业新高地建设，深化国资国企改革、坚持走新型工业化道路、保持快速持续协调平稳发展态势的历程。在此基础上，对2006年上海工业发展环境和聚焦点作了预期展望。

2. 重点反映了上海工业企业自主创新的进展情况

《报告》以反映产业技术创新水平为主线，突出反映了上海提升企业自主创新能力的进展情况和最新趋势，体现了国家战略、上海科教兴市主战略，顺应了上海构建以自主创新为核心的城市创新体系的发展要求，概述了上海工业"十五"期间创新工作做法和2005年的重点企业的推进举措。报告对重点行业的创新情况作了描述。

3. 重点反映了上海工业行业在全国的地位

《报告》采用点、面结合的方式，点上涉及装备、信息、汽车、石油化工和精细化工、精品钢材以及战略产业、新兴产业、都市工业等。面上涉及上海和国内其他地区的对比分析。通过省市和行业的产值、利润等指标的综合分析，客观真实地展现了上海工业的发展阶段和在全国所处的地位。

本《报告》在编写过程中，得到了市政府有关部门和社会有关各方的大力帮助。由于我们经验、能力和积累有限，难免有疏漏之处，敬请社会各界鉴谅并指正。

编 者

目 录

第一章 总报告

一、上海工业发展回顾 / 003

二、2006 年上海工业发展环境分析 / 011

三、2006 年上海工业发展的聚焦点 / 012

第二章 装备制造业

一、上海"十五"期间行业发展结构特点 / 017

二、2005 年总体运行情况 / 018

三、行业科技投入情况 / 019

四、2006 年预测 / 020

第三章 电子信息产品制造业

一、"十五"期间行业发展结构特点 / 023

二、2005 年总体运行现状 / 024

三、行业科技投入情况 / 025

四、2006 年发展预测 / 026

第四章 汽车产业

一、"十五"期间行业发展结构特点 / 029

二、2005 年总体运行现状 / 031

三、行业科技投入情况 / 032

四、2006 年发展预测 / 033

第五章 石油化工及精细化工业

一、"十五"期间行业发展结构特点 / 037

二、2005 年行业总体运行现状 / 038

三、行业科技投入情况 / 039

四、2006 年发展预测 / 039

第六章 精品钢材制造业

一、"十五"期间行业发展结构特点 / 043

二、2005 年总体运行现状 / 043

三、行业科技投入情况 / 044

四、2006 年发展预测 / 045

第七章 战略产业

一、船舶产业 / 049

二、海洋装备产业 / 051

三、航空航天产业 / 052

第八章 新兴产业

一、生物医药制造业 / 057

二、新能源产业 / 059

三、生产性服务业 / 060

第九章 都市工业

一、"十五"期间行业发展结构类型 / 065

二、2005 年行业总体运行状况 / 066

三、2006 年发展预测 / 067

第十章 工业能源消费状况

一、"十五"期间上海工业能耗总体状况 / 071

二、存在的问题 / 073

三、2006 年发展预测 / 073

附件 1 2005 年上海工业及技术创新大事记 / 075

附件 2 上海工业 1990 年~2005 年主要数据一览表 / 078

附件 3 2005 年区县工业主要工业经济指标统计表 / 079

Part I General

第 一 章

总 报 告

"十五"期间，在党中央、国务院一系列方针政策指引下，在市委、市政府的正确领导下，上海工业由20世纪90年代"在调整中发展"转向"在发展中调整"，大力推进产业结构的战略性调整，深化国有企业改革重组，加快工业新高地建设；贯彻"两个优先"产业发展方针，探索二、三产业联动发展，使先进制造业和现代服务业"并驾齐驱"，不仅完成了既定的"十五"发展目标和任务，而且保持了持续、快速、健康增长的势头，为全市经济连续14年保持两位数增长发挥了重要作用，也为"十一五"发展迈向更高的台阶、2006年"开好局，起好步"奠定了扎实的基础。

一、上海工业发展回顾

（一）"十五"期间工业发展回顾

"十五"期间，上海工业认真实践科学发展观，全面落实科教兴国的国家战略和科教兴市主战略，坚持走新型工业化道路，强化创新、提升能级、发展装备、建设基地，较好地完成了"十五"预定的各项经济指标，取得了明显成效。

1. 工业支撑带动作用增强

"十五"期间，上海工业继续保持较快的增长态势，发挥着对全市经济的重要支撑作用。工业总产值在五年中增长了近1万亿元，年均增长18.9%；2005年全市工业完成工业总产值16876.8亿元，其中规模以上口径（下同）工业企业实现工业总产值15806.78亿元，比2000年增长1.4倍。工业增加值五年中翻了一番多，年均递增15.4%（见图1.1）。"十五"期间工业总量是前50年上海工业总量之和。"十五"期间，上海工业对全市经济增长的贡献率达到53.2%，成为拉动全市经济增长的重要力量。

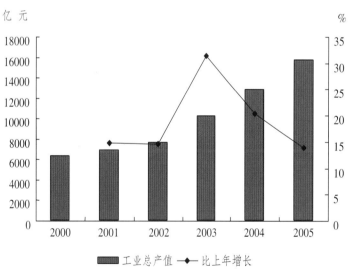

图1.1 "十五"期间上海工业总产值及增速

2. 创新驱动发展作用凸显

本世纪以前，上海经济持续增长主要依靠投资驱动，每年工业投资总额基本保持在全社会固定资产投资的1/3。随着经济增长方式的转变，创新已成为支撑工业发展的重要力量。"十五"期间，全社会科技研发（R&D）投入翻了一番以上，占全市GDP比例从1.69%提高到2.34%，其中，企业研发投入占全社会研发总投入的62%。目前世界上主要发达国家的R&D投入普遍在2%以上。上海已在全国率先超出国际惯例2%，踏入创新驱动期"门槛"。"十五"期间，上海工业企业R&D经费投入增长年均增幅达29.9％，是增长最快的时期。2005年，上海规模以上工业企业共投入R&D经费120.8亿元，比2000年增长2.7倍，年均增长29.9％，其中大中型工业企业R&D经费投入达108.4亿元，增长2.5倍，年均增长28.5％。企业R&D经费投入的快速增长，使全社会R&D经费投入结构发生了明显变化，2005年上海规模以上工业企业R&D经费投入占全市R&D投入总量的56.6％，比2000年提高13.8个百分点。以企业为主体的研发体系正在不断形成和完善之中，企业R&D投入明显向高技术产业和六大工业重点发展行业集聚，2005年，上海高技术产业R&D经费投入达到38.3亿元，比2000年增长2倍，年均增长24.5％。六大工业重点发展行业R&D经费投入达到104.8亿元，增长2.7倍，年均增长30.1％，占全市工业R&D投入的比重达到86.8％，其中，从总量来看，2005年居前三位的行业是轿车制造业占33.9％、信息产品制造业占32.4％和成套设备制造业占17.7％；从增长速度来看，2005年比2000年增长居前三位的行业是轿车制造业4.9倍、成套设备制造业3.3倍和信息产品制造业2.5倍（见表1.1）。

表1.1 全市六大工业重点发展行业R&D经费投入及比重

行 业	2000 年		2005 年	
	R&D经费投入（亿元）	比重（％）	R&D经费投入（亿元）	比重（％）
合 计	28.11	100	104.83	100
信息产品制造业	9.73	34.6	33.95	32.4
轿车制造业	5.99	21.3	35.58	33.9
石油化工及精细化工制造业	2.85	10.1	4.81	4.6
精品钢材制造业	2.84	10.1	7.89	7.5
成套设备制造业	4.35	15.5	18.51	17.7
生物医药制造业	2.35	8.4	4.09	3.9

国家级、市级企业技术中心队伍不断扩大，分别由"九五"末期的23家和57家增加的到2005年的29家和160家。在全市1000多家规模以上工业企业中，这189家市级以上企业技术中心所在企业的从业人员数仅占21.10％，产品销售收入却占35.3％，利润占79.8％；研究与试验发展经费支出约占全市的49.5％，专利申请数占全市的19.1％，发明专利申请数占全市的34.3％；与高校等外单位合建开发机构总数达193家，设在海外的开发机构数达42家，全年产学研合作经费支出达25.7亿元。同时，外资在上海设立的研发中心增加到170家，其中汽巴精化、思科、圣戈班等跨国公司将其从事基础研发的全球研发中心设在上海。上海工业企业加速自主创新的活力和动力倍增。

上海工业创新成果不断涌现，增长方式逐步由单一的投资驱动向投资、创新驱动并举转型。以市场为导向的自主创新格局初步形成。2005年，上海规模以上工业企业新产品产值达3408.8亿元，为2000年的2.4倍，年均增长19.4％，占工业总产值的21.6％；新产品实现销售收入3429.4亿元，为2000年的2.4倍，年均增长19.6％，占21％。2005年，上海工业企业专利申请量为2.3万件，比2000年增长近2倍，占全市专利申请总量的69.9％；工业企业专利授权量为8486件，增长3倍，占全市专利授权总量的67.3％。随着上海工业企业自主创新能力的不断增强，目前引进国外技术经费支出与R&D经费支出之比已由2000年的1.20:1下降到2005年的0.38:1，工业增长的集约化程度不断提高，工业万元增加值能耗逐年下降，工业对环境的友好度大幅提高，发展潜力不断增强。

3. 产业结构能级明显提升

"十五"期间，上海工业抓住国际产业转移机遇，加快产业结构优化升级。六大支柱产业产值占全市工业的比重由"九五"末期的48.6%提高到63.4%。高新技术产业快速增长，已经形成一定规模并逐步成为上海工业的主导产业，其产值比重占全市工业总产值比重逐年上升，由2000年末的20.6%提高到2004年的28.2%。电子信息产业成为工业的第一支柱产业，年均增长34%，占全市工业的25.5%，是拉动全市工业产出增长的重要力量。石化、钢铁等基础产业改造升级步伐加快，并逐步实现与高新技术产业的融合。轻重工业比重基本稳定在3:7的水平，与国际上典型的重化工业中后期的特征基本吻合，表明上海工业正处于重化工业持续稳定的增长期，上海工业结构正在向高能级、带动型方向迈进。

4. 工业投资结构不断优化

"十五"期间，上海工业总投资约为4216亿元，年度投资额基本保持在全社会固定资产投资的1/3，且结构日趋合理。工业投资更加向优势行业和重点产业基地集中，五年中六大支柱产业总投资约2600亿元，占工业总投资的61%左右。"十五"期间外资投资占全市工业投资的28%左右，民间投资占工业投资的比重提高到15%。此外，通过实施"走出去"和服务全国战略，"十五"期间上海工业的市外投资开始加快步伐，规模达到200亿元左右，其总量已占到本地投资的5%左右，引领上海产品不断走向国际市场。"十五"期间，全市工业外向度（出口交货值占工业总产值的比重）不断提高，2005达31.5%，比2000年提高11个百分点。

5. 产业布局调整成绩显著

"十五"期间，上海继续对工业布局进行大规模调整，以郊区为主，工业重心向郊区转移，制造业向工业园区集中，推动工业从600平方公里向6000平方公里的市域范围拓展。一是加快产业基地和开发区建设步伐。在巩固精品钢材产业基地的同时，重点推进汽车、石化和微电子产业基地建设，在"十五"期末又适时启动了临港装备和长兴造船两大产业基地建设。同时，确立了重点建设市级以上工业区的战略目标。目前六大产业基地和市级以上工业区的总产出已占到全市的50%以上。二是结合城市功能变化，盘活中心城区老工业厂房等存量资源，大力建设都市型工业园和创意产业园区。积极发展广就业、环保型的都市产业。提高资源整合，促进二三产联动，截至2005年底，共建设230个都市型工业园区（楼宇），30个创意产业园区，盘活400多万平方米老工业厂房，吸纳70万人就业。三是大力推进工业向园区集中，打造以产业链为基础的产业集群。据统计，六大产业基地和市级以上工业园区的工业集中度达到了50%。"十五"期末，上海对开发区进行了调整，国家级工业区增加到5个（外高桥保税区、金桥出口加工区、张江高科技园区、漕河泾新兴技术开发区和闵行经济技术开发区）和市级工业区增加到13个。

（二）2005年工业发展特点

1. 产业规模总量持续增长

2005年全市工业生产保持稳定增长。工业总产值达15806.8亿元，比上年增长13.9%。规模以上工业企业达到1.5万家，资产总计为15893.4亿元，从业人员数为258.2万人，全年完成主营业务收入16346.1亿元。

从隶属关系看，区县工业逾"半壁江山"，实现总产值占全市工业的58%；中央工业占21.8%，主要地方工业（即电气、汽车、华谊、广电、仪电、轻工、纺织、建材、医药、有色、计算机等市属的11个集团）占17.4%（见表1.2）。

表 1.2 2005 年分隶属关系主要经济指标完成情况

单位：亿元

指标	类别	规模以上	中央企业	主要地方工业	区县工业	其他
资产总量	数量	15893.4	4557.3	3141	7311.5	883.6
	占比	-	28.7%	19.8%	46%	5.6%
总产值	数量	15806.8	3443	2752.1	9175.3	436.3
	占比	-	21.8%	17.4%	58%	2.8%
销售收入	数量	16316.1	3631.5	2936.2	9279.8	498.6
	占比	-	22.2%	18%	56.8%	3.1%
利润	数量	939.6	323.6	174.3	391.2	50.5
	占比	-	34.4%	18.6%	41.6%	5.4%

从主要行业看，电子、机械行业实现工业总产值分别占全市 22% 和 19.8%，轻工、石化、冶金、汽车合计占 43.4%，其他行业占 24.8%（见表 1.3）。

表 1.3 2005 年主要行业经济指标完成情况

单位：亿元

指标	类别	规模以上	电子	机械	化工	石化	冶金	汽车
资产总量	数量	15893.4	2421.28	2947.84	2397.32	1562.50	1743.80	1148.58
	占比	-	15.2%	18.5%	15.1%	9.8%	11.0%	7.2%
总产值	数量	15806.8	3473.69	3134.83	2574.29	1892.66	1339.84	1043.06
	占比	-	22.0%	19.8%	16.3%	12.0%	8.5%	6.6%
销售收入	数量	16316.1	3538.49	3158.24	2648.64	1890.73	1488.87	1186.81
	占比	-	21.6%	19.3%	16.2%	11.6%	9.1%	7.3%
利润	数量	939.6	54.36	226.04	129.87	67.26	178.33	99.58
	占比	-	5.8%	24.1%	13.8%	7.2%	19.0%	10.6%

从所有制情况看，外资经济实现工业总产值占全市 62.2%，股份制经济占 27.7%，其余各所制经济占 10.1%（见表 1.4）。

表 1.4 2005 年各所有制经济主要经济指标完成情况

单位：亿元

指标	类别	纺织	电力	建材	有色	医药	烟草	其他
资产总量	数量	693.17	1161.75	320.61	152.03	304.18	421.42	618.95
	占比	4.4%	7.3%	2.0%	1.0%	1.9%	2.7%	3.9%
总产值	数量	775.12	565.71	261.89	256.01	216.86	215.70	57.13
	占比	4.9%	3.6%	1.7%	1.6%	1.4%	1.4%	0.4%
销售收入	数量	768.83	577.02	262.96	260.79	228.06	226.95	109.73
	占比	4.7%	3.5%	1.6%	1.6%	1.4%	1.4%	0.7%
利润	数量	31.79	41.13	9.90	8.64	15.86	71.10	5.70
	占比	3.4%	4.4%	1.1%	0.9%	1.7%	7.6%	0.6%

2. 企业技术创新力度加大

（1）科研投入情况。2005年，上海工业企业科研开发投入261.1亿元，比上年增长12.6%。其中用于研究与开发活动（R&D）经费支出达到120.8亿元，增长30.2%，占科研投入的45.3%。科研投入强度（科研开发投入占主营业务收入的比重）达到1.6%。高技术产业产值占全市工业比重25.1%。高技术产业自主知识产权拥有率为27.5%，比上年提高0.6个百分点。2005年末，全市工业企业共有科技人员7.6万人，科研机构479个。外商及港澳台投资科研开发投入最多，达175.3亿元，占全市工业的65.7%，比其主营业务收入所占比重高3.8个百分点。其中用于研究与试验发展活动经费支出为90.9亿元，占科研投入的51.9%。其科研开发投入强度为1.7%。

（2）重点项目情况。积极推进列入网络软件交换平台、可降解纤维材料、煤液化成套设备等首批科教兴市重大产业化攻关项目的实施，实际投入4.7亿元，其中科教兴市重大项目资金投入2.8亿元，锻炼了一批创新团队，在核心技术和关键技术方面形成了一批自主知识产权，其中，申请（包括已授权）中国专利94项，申请（包括已授权）外国专利15项，获得版权3项，注册商标32个。项目总体进展情况良好，其中平底船已投入外高桥与洋山港之间江海联运应用。神华煤直接液化6吨/天中试装置在上海进行了第二次长周期试验，实现连续投煤成功运行18天。船用半组合曲轴生产基地在上海建成投产，形成了具有自主知识产权的核心制造技术，打破了国外企业的垄断。超大型船舶柴油机等9个项目被列入第二批重大产业化攻关专项。

（3）自主产权情况。全年企业申请专利2.2万件，占全市申请量的69%，继续发挥主体作用。有134项专利新产品被认定为"2005年上海市专利新产品"；有29家企业被确认为"上海市知识产权示范企业（培育企业）"。93个项目被列入"上海市吸收与创新计划"，包括"平板显示驱动芯片"在内的11个项目被列入第二批"促进整机业与集成电路设计业联动专项"。加快了以企业为主体、以自主创新为核心的技术创新体系建设。全市新增市级企业技术中心38家、国家级企业技术中心1家、国家级分中心2家；新增区级企业技术中心84家。

3. 工业投资保持适度增长

在2004年比上年增长25.1%的基础上，2005年工业投资完成1074.8亿元，同比增长7.3%，这是"十五"计划以来投资增幅较为平缓的一年。从全市固定资产投资情况来看，基本保持着15%左右的增幅，基础设施投资大幅增长（25%以上），房地产投资保持10%以上的增幅，工业投资占全市投资的比重为30.3%（见图1.2）。

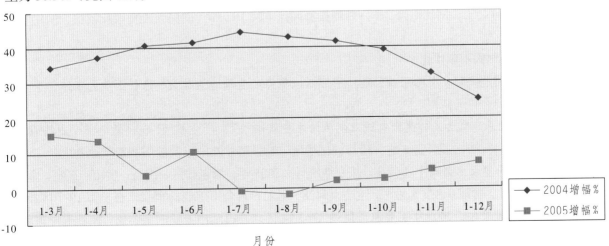

图 1.2 2004 年和 2005 年工业投资增幅比较图

从投资结构看，六大支柱产业投资628.3亿元，占全市工业投资总量的比重为58.5%。其中，装备制造业增幅最快，投资达142.8亿元，增幅205%；钢铁产业投资140亿元，同比增长52.4%；汽车产业投资80亿元，同比增长22.6%；石化产业投资111.4亿元，同比下降41.9%；电子信息产业投资142.4亿元，同比下降31.8%；生物医药产业投资18亿元，同比下降7%（见图1.3）。

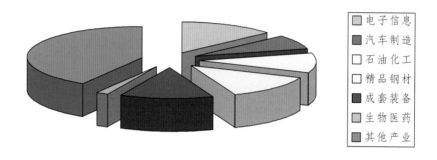

图1.3 六大支柱工业投资结构分布图

从投资重点看，2005年投资重点主要是结构调整和产业升级项目。装备产业主要在提高上海机电行业总体装备水平和极端制造能力，主要项目有总投资32亿元的电气临港重装备基地项目、上重厂大型铸锻件扩大产能项目、总投资17亿元的沪东中华造船（集团）有限公司船用柴油机项目；石化产业主要是具有世界级规模的百万吨级乙烯及异氰酸酯、苯酚丙酮、聚氯乙烯等相关产业项目；电子信息主要的投资方向是生产8英寸0.25微米以下集成电路的生产线及后封装项目；钢铁主要是填补国内空白的宽厚板生产线，替代进口的不锈钢冷、热轧生产线等结构调整项目；汽车主要是开发新产品的大众三厂改造、通用扩产项目。投资项目具有产业关联度大、技术水平高、具有当今国际领先水平的特征。

从投资规模看，2005年项目投资向规模化发展。确定总投资20亿元以上的重点项目20项，到年底建成了6项，有宝钢股份总投资68亿元的5米宽厚板项目、总投资74亿元的1800冷轧带钢项目、总投资35.6亿元的宝钢不锈钢二期扩建项目、总投资28.8亿元的通用汽车二期扩建项目、总投资224亿元的上海赛科90万吨乙烯等6个项目。

从所有制分类看，2005年国有经济投资保持增长态势，非国有经济投资有所下降。按照所有制分类，国有经济投资348亿元，占工业投资总量的三分之一左右，同比增长33.4%，非国有经济投资732亿元，占总量的三分之二，同比下降2%，外商投资同比下降19.7%。而民间投资增长较快，同比增长38.9%。

4. 产业布局结构不断优化

经过持续不断地调整，上海工业已初步形成了以重点产业基地为龙头、区县工业为主体、工业园区为重要载体的产业布局结构。

（1）六大产业基地成为支撑先进制造业发展的主要载体。六大产业基地，包括微电子产业基地、汽车制造产业基地、石油化工产业基地、精品钢材基地、装备产业基地以及船舶制造产业基地。

（2）工业布局重点主要集中在郊区。按在地统计，2005年，浦东新区、闵行、宝山、嘉定、金山、南汇、奉贤、松江、青浦9个区工业总产值达13428.3亿元，占全市工业的85%。在全市19个区县中，浦东新区工业总量最大，2005年工业总产值达3763.14亿元，占全市工业的23.8%。工业总产值超过2000亿元的还有闵行区和松江区，超过1000亿元的有宝山区、嘉定区。发展速度最快的是松江区，增幅达36.7%，闵行区达到25.7%。

（3）"工业向园区集中"取得突破性进展。2005年国家级和市级工业区实现工业总产值6916亿元，比上年同期增长43.8%。上海松江出口加工区以1132.18亿元工业总产值、52%的增幅位居各工业开发区之首。工业总产值超过1000亿元的开发区2个，500亿元到1000亿元的2个，200亿元到500亿元的6个。2005年工业集中度（含六大产业基地）从49%提高到53%。工业区主导产业集聚度进一步提高，市级以上工业区的主导产业集聚度达到80%以上。在工业区内形成了以若干产业集群为核心的发展态势，如闵行开发区形成了机电、医药医疗、食品饮料三大产业集群；在漕河泾形成了电子信息、新材料、生物医药、航空航天等产业集群；在金桥开发区形成电子信息、汽车及零部件、现代家电等产业集群；松江工业区以计算机制造为主的电子信息产业得到快速发展。产业集聚效应进一步显现，工业开发区内的通信设备、计算机及其他电子设备制造业完成主营业务收入3158.54亿元，占全市该行业的89.3%；仪器仪表及文化、办公用机械制造业完成主营业务收入占全市该行业的73.5%；交通运输设备制造业、电气机械及器材制造业、化学原料及化学制品制造业的主营业务收入占全市该行业的比重均超过40%。

5. 对外开放度不断提升

2005年，上海工业企业出口交货值继续保持快速增长，共完成4990.9亿元，比上年增长29.2%，增幅大大高于全市工业总产值；出口交货值超过100亿元的有10个行业，其中通用设备制造业、交通运输设备制造业，电气机械及器材制造业，通信设备、计算机及其他电子设备制造业4个行业出口交货值达200亿元以上。

出口交货值增幅超过50%的有木材加工及木竹藤棕草制品业、塑料制品业、通用设备制造业、专用设备制造业，其中专用设备制造业增速最高，为61.3%。

拥有"上海松江出口加工区"的松江和拥有"外高桥保税区"、"金桥出口加工区"的浦东新区是上海重要的工业出口基地，2005年出口交货值分别完成1372亿元和1209.8亿元，共占全市工业出口交货值的51.9%。

外商及港澳台投资经济成为出口主力，2005年完成出口交货值4415.3亿元，占全市工业出口的88.6%。

（三）全国地位比较分析

1. 上海工业在全国曾长期居于举足轻重的地位。

然而随着各地经济快速发展，"十五"期间上海在全国位次有所下降。2005年，上海工业生产总量在全国列第五位，比2000年下降一位；排名前四位的是：广东、江苏、山东、浙江。上海工业生产总量占全国比重由7.2%降至6%；主营业务收入占全国的6.7%，利润总额占6.5%，出口交货值占10.4%。

2. 部分兄弟省市工业发展特点

（1）广东省生产总量一直位居全国前列。目前已与其他省市在全国位次拉开了较大距离。2005年，完成主营业务收入34033.3亿元，比上年增长27.5%；实现利润总额1457.6亿元。广东工业发展的特点是，通信设备、计算机及其他电子设备制造业独领风骚，其余各行业全面发展。广东省全年通信设备、计算机及其他电子设备制造业主营业务收入达9351.2亿元，占全省主营业务收入的27.5%，比第二位的江苏省多4106.3亿元，比上海多5812.7亿元。

（2）江苏省依靠大行业，保持良好的发展势头。2005年江苏省完成主营业务收入32129.5亿元，比上年增长28.8%；实现利润1386.5亿元。其特点在于整体规模大的行业多，主营业务收入超过千亿元的工业行业有7个，即纺织业，化学原料及化学制品制造业，黑色金属冶炼及压延加工业，通用设备制造业，电气机械及器材制造业，交通运输设备制造业，通信设备、计算机及其他电子设备制造业。这些行业发展势头好，从而带动了全省工业经济的发展。

（3）山东省凭藉资源优势实现加速发展。2005年山东省完成主营业务收入29910.8亿元，比上年增长43%；实现利润2138.2亿元。山东省工业发展的特点在于：采矿业发达，出产原油，国际原油价格上涨对其非常有利，同时上海失去优势的传统产业（如纺织业）在山东发展迅速。2005年，山东省多数工业行业效益提高，基础性行业优势突出。在39个工业行业中，有38个行业实现利润比上年增长，实现利润在100亿元以上且增幅较高的行业有6个，即石油和天然气开采业增长76.3%，纺织业增长76.2%，化学原料及化学制品制造业增长68.5%，农副食品加工业增长67.8%，煤炭开采和洗选业增长47.8%，非金属矿物制品业增长40.7%；实现利润在50亿～100亿元的行业有7个。

（4）浙江省民营经济发达、行业发展均衡。2005年浙江省完成主营业务收入21702.5亿元，增长24.7%；实现利润1072.8亿元。浙江省以私营企业为主，私营工业企业主营业务收入占规模以上工业企业比重为34.6%，对全省工业利税、利润增长的贡献率分别达到43.7%和49.4%，拉动利税、利润增长5.9个和5.7个百分点。行业发展均衡也是浙江工业的一个特点，由于没有规模超大的行业，单个行业变化不会对整体工业产生大的影响，并且有七成以上的行业经营业绩好于全国同行，使得全省工业经济保持良好的运行态势。

3. 投资增幅下降是上海工业全国位次有所下降的首要原因。

从发展后劲来看，近两年，上海工业固定资产投资增幅远远低于全国工业领先的四个省份。投资对工业拉动作用减弱，导致上海工业生产增速放慢，并直接影响到今后工业发展后劲。2005年，上海工业固定资产投资1074.8亿元，比上年仅增长7.3%，占全社会固定资产投资的比重比上年回落2.2个百分点，其中六个重点发展行业投资628.4亿元，仅增长1.4%（见表1.5）。

表1.5　　近两年五省市工业固定资产投资额比较

单位：亿元

指　标	2004 年	增长（%）	2005 年	增长（%）
上海	1001.2	25.1	1074.8	7.3
山东	2816	34.3	4007.2	42.3
江苏	2101.92	26.2	2765.2	31.6
浙江	2704.7	35.3	2942.5	22.4
广东	1639.02	31.4	2722.8	32.1

（上表中上海、山东、江苏以及广东省2004年数据口径为城镇以上，浙江、广东省2005年数据口径为限额以上）

（四）"十五"能源供应状况

"十五"期间，电力、煤炭、原油的供应及其价格变化，对上海工业生产和经济运行带来一定的压力。

1. 电力

在全国经济发展速度加快，各地均出现了电力、煤炭供应紧张大背景下，因煤炭供应趋紧、发电能力有限，外购电力难度加大，再加上上海连续几年夏季高温期长、用电负荷屡创历史新高等因素，"十五"期间，上海电力供应矛盾比较突出。夏季高温期间，为保证城市电力正常供应和工业企业正常生产，采取了电力迎峰度夏的各项措施，精心实施企业高温期生产让电计划，从而把电力供应矛盾对上海工业生产的影响降到了最低程度。

2. 煤炭

上海曾数度出现库存量大幅下降，供应告急情况，再加上煤炭价格大幅度上涨，既增加了生产组织难度，也导致生产成本增加。

3. 原油

因受中东局势动荡的影响，国际市场原油价格持续上涨，对上海工业企业生产影响较大。作为上海重点发展行业之一的石油化工和精细化工制造业，其最基本的加工原料是石油，受影响最大，部分下游产品出现了停产或减产的现象，多数生产企业利润严重下降，有些严重亏损。

4. 天然气

"十五"期间，"四气东输"开始启动。但因前期对天然气供应量预期过大，而实际到位数明显少于计划供应量，因此对上海工业生产带来不利影响。天然气供应只能以保证居民生活用气为主，导致一些以天然气为主要能源的工业企业被迫陷入停产的困境。

由于市委、市政府及时采取措施，能源矛盾正在逐步缓解，影响限制在最低程度。

二、2006 年上海工业发展环境分析

1. 世界经济走势

国际机构对 2006 年全球经济谨慎看好。全球经济增长预期将延续 2005 年轨迹，基本持平，维持中等增长速度。高收入国家经济将保持平稳运行，主要得益于美、欧、日三大经济体经济的稳定增长，美国经济仍然是世界经济增长的主要动力。大多数发展中国家经济增长会高于世界平均水平，中国、印度及其他一些发展中国家对世界经济增长的影响日趋重要。世界贸易将继续呈现活跃趋势，继续维持较高的增长水平。

构成世界经济增长威胁的不确定因素主要有：全球金融失衡、油价继续大幅上升、禽流感转向人类感染，以及一些主要经济体房地产市场过热可能导致房地产价格的剧烈下跌等。2006 年，全球国际收支面临失衡，美国巨额的经常账户逆差和迅速上升的净对外债务可能导致美元恶性贬值，世界经济将受到较大负面冲击，不少发展中国家面临货币升值压力和外汇储备上升所带来的政策难题。短期内国际石油市场供求仍然偏紧张，世界范围的通货膨胀率将有所上涨，但由于能源价格上涨向总体价格的转移有限，通货膨胀率的预期仍较低且较平稳。当然，如果能源价格居高不下，或继续上扬，通货膨胀率上涨的压力会愈来愈大。贸易保护主义和贸易摩擦的现象仍有所抬头，非关税贸易壁垒在世界范围有所上升，将在一定程度上抵销关税减免带来的刺激世界贸易增长的动力。

2. 国内政策环境

2006 年中国经济将保持平稳较快增长的良好趋势。国家将继续加强和改善宏观调控，保持宏观经济政策的连续性和稳定性，继续实行稳健的财政政策和货币政策。同时，国家将对新情况新问题进行适度微调，把经济发展的着力点放到调整经济结构、转变经济增长方式、提高经济效益上来，保持经济增长速度适宜，实现发展又快又好。

扩大内需作为我国经济发展的长期战略方针和基本立足点，2006 年将放到更加重要的位置。按照建设社会主义新农村的要求，国家将致力于有效地启动农村市场，把增加居民消费，特别是农民消费作为扩大消费需求的重点，转变投资投向，实行由城市建设为主向更多地重视农村建设的重大转变。

宏观调控将继续把好土地、信贷两个闸门，防止投资膨胀反弹，并推动部分产能过剩行业调整，对不符合产业政策和市场准入条件，国家明令淘汰的项目和企业，国家进一步采取措施，加大力度，从严控制，有步骤解决。

为落实国家中长期科技发展规划纲要，建设创新型国家，2006 年国家将加大对自主创新的支持力度，财政科技支出将比上年增长 19.2%，明显高于财政收入和支出的增幅，并将通过税收抵扣、减免和加速

折旧等税收优惠政策以及政府采购政策，营造激励创新的环境，推动企业成为创新主体，促进科技进步。

国企改革、商业银行股份制改革和股权分置改革是 2006 年的一个重头戏，石油、天然气等资源性产品价格改革将提上日程。为了使节约能源资源务必取得明显成效，钢铁、有色、电力、建材等高耗能行业和企业，将依法强制淘汰落后技术、工艺和产品。

环境保护将得到进一步重视，并纳入地方政府和领导干部考核的重要内容，定期公布考核结果。

3. 上海自身发展环境

2006 年是实施"十一五规划"的第一年。上海工业将围绕增强城市国际竞争力，向创新驱动发展的道路转型，进一步转变增长方式和增长动力。

（1）企业自主创新进入新阶段。上海将根据国家有关政策，结合上海实际，落实相关政策细则，聚焦重点领域，突破关键瓶颈，加快落实科学发展观，大力实施科教兴市主战略，形成以企业为主体、市场为导向、产学研相结合的技术创新体系，完善企业创新的激励机制，引导上海企业走自主创新道路。

（2）上海新郊区建设将得到全面推进。建设具有国际大都市特点的现代化新郊区，是"十一五"期间上海发展的重要内容。2006 年上海将重点推进农业现代化，加快现代化郊区城镇建设，全面推进农村综合改革，郊区产业发展以及规划、人口、环境等方面将得到全面的重视。

（3）能源供应和安全将引起特别关注。能源和环保列入"十一五"规划的重要目标，上海面临着要在"十一五"期末单位 GDP 能耗降低 20% 的艰巨任务。上海在节约能源方面，与发达国家相比，差距大、潜力也大。电力供求的缺口减小，石油供应受计划控制，天然气供应不足成为主要矛盾。2006 年将采取更加有力的措施，坚持开发节约并重、节约优先，确保能源供应和能源安全。

（4）改革开放面临新机遇。浦东新区综合配套改革试点是中央赋予上海的一个千载难逢的发展契机。2006 年上海将在发挥浦东改革先发效应，实现浦东与浦西联动方面形成实质性突破。2006 年上海将基本完成控股公司三年改革的目标和任务，全面完成国有控股上市公司的股权分置改革，上海国资国企改革将得到更好的体制环境和发展空间。在中国"入世"五年过渡期的最后一年，上海将利用服务贸易对外开放上的先发效应，在金融、贸易、制造等领域，吸引更多的跨国公司在上海设立地区总部、营运中心和研发中心。

（5）加快发展现代服务业。2006 年上海将不断开拓工作思路，创新工作方法，加大发展现代服务业力度，以现代服务业集聚区建设为突破口，大力发展金融业、物流业、创意产业、生产性服务业等，在形成服务经济为主的产业结构方面取得新进展、新突破。

（6）一批"十一五"重大基础设施和重点发展项目进入投资建设期。世博项目将全面启动，轨道交通进入高峰建设期，机场改扩建、洋山港后续工程等投资量大的项目也将陆续开工。2006 年工业投资将保持一定的增长水平，增幅与上年略有增长。钢铁项目、集成电路项目开始新一轮建设、新能源汽车项目、重大国产化装备自主制造装备制造业项目等一批对产业升级和科教兴市带动和支撑作用明显的投资将得到政策倾斜。

三、2006 年上海工业发展的聚焦点

1. 切实加强经济运行调节

完善以"预测、预警、预案、预控"为工作抓手，确保全年两个"两位数增长"。以年产值 1000 亿元以上的电子、机械、轻工、石化、冶金、汽车等 6 个行业为重点行业；以年销售 2 亿元的中芯国际、比亚迪电子、振华港机、广电 NEC、凯泉泵业等 20 户各种所有制企业为重点企业；以液晶显示屏、平板电视、集成电路、轿车、空调压缩机、成品钢材、成品油、乙烯、轮胎外胎、机床等 21 个产品为重

点产品；以工业产出1000亿元左右的松江、闵行、浦东、嘉定等4个区为重点区域，加强动态跟踪。预测做细，进一步完善月度工业生产预测网络和季度工业效益预测网络，跟踪国家重大政策的出台和国际、国内重大事件和热点问题，进一步完善经济运行分析、重点产品进出口和市场价格、产业安全预警等3个监测网络。调控做实，确保上海煤电气等重要能源、原材料的稳定供应，努力确保煤炭库存在14天以上、成品油库存在7天以上，实现紧急情况下的资源稳定供应。

2. 努力增强企业创新能力

围绕"聚焦企业主体、提高创新能力"的目标，采取切实措施，力争用3～5年时间使全市企业创新能力明显提高。 一是推进重大装备自主创新。积极贯彻国务院《关于加快振兴装备制造业的若干意见》，制定上海《关于加快重大技术装备自主创新的实施细则》，市有关部门形成协调机制，按照经济规律和市场规则，通过对用户和制造企业的支持鼓励，形成风险共担机制，突破重大技术装备首台业绩，实现重大工程与重大技术装备联动。二是推动产学研战略联盟。发挥企业在产学研合作中的主导作用，在重大产业化项目中，企业要成为技术创新项目的提出者，推动创新项目产业化和创新成果商业化。鼓励产学研紧密合作，建立各类技术创新联合组织，研发机构要成为项目研究和科技攻关的主要力量。整合和构筑产学研信息沟通平台，加强协调机制，推动产学研联合。三是提高企业创新投入。帮助企业落实国家和上海鼓励企业创新的各项政策，支持企业加大研发投入，支持承担国家重大产业化科技攻关项目。加大政府对企业创新的支持力度，发挥财政资金对企业创新的激励作用和放大作用，鼓励有条件的企业购买先进技术和研发装备、测试仪器。鼓励企业提高融资能力，利用资上海场融资，不断拓展融资渠道。四是推进工业区成为企业创新的载体。在全市开展若干个园区试点，建立面向产业的技术服务平台，完善产业技术情报信息系统，构筑为企业创新服务的开放体系。重点搭建微电子、系统软件、中药现代化、生物工程、纳米技术、通信技术、新材料等先进制造业共性和公共技术平台。在漕河泾新兴技术开发区、上海化工区、国际汽车城、临港产业区和莘庄等条件较好的工业区试点推进。五是引进和培育技术创新人才。推进"万、千、百、十"人才发展计划，着重突出培养和吸引技术创新的领军人物、学科带头人、科技骨干和技术工人。鼓励有条件的企业设立首席技术官，提高技术人员在企业领导班子中的地位。发挥专业技术人员和技术工人在企业创新中的积极作用。

3. 大力推进产业基地建设

2006年重点推进6个100亿元以上重大项目建设、20个20亿元以上重点产业升级项目建设、10个装备业战略升级项目、10个现代物流业建设项目，总投资达1500多亿元，项目建成后预计新增销售收入2000多亿元，并在2006年建成投产1/3以上。主要有宝钢汽车板硅钢生产线、罗泾COREX、一钢不锈钢冷轧项目；化工区拜耳聚碳酸脂、联合异氰酸脂、华胜化工烧碱氯乙烯项目；上广电NEC第五代TFT二期，中芯国际深亚微米集成电路项目；上汽工程研究院项目；电气临港装备基地等。一是完善投资项目库。按照"开工一批、投产一批、储备一批"的原则，充实和完善投资建设项目储备库，结合项目备案、核准管理办法，完善项目库电子网络。做好投资分析、项目用地需求分析等，编制2006～2008年三年滚动计划。二是加大重大项目的协调力度。建立重大项目的协调机制，加强政府有关部门的沟通联系，建立重大项目绿色通道，加快项目建设进度，保持上海工业的增长后劲。制订推进上海重点投资项目管理办法，对列入重点项目的要求、程序、支持政策、土地政策和相应的服务内容形成规范，对重点项目建设做到"四个优先"，即优先列入上海市重大项目、优先列入重点协调、优先保证供地、优先提供资金支持。三是引导企业加快产业结构调整。针对目前上海土地资源紧张、实现自主创新的情况，通过政府优惠政策（如贴息等）的支持，鼓励企业进行技术改造、技术引进，优化产业结构，提高企业竞争力，提升产业能级，走可持续发展的道路。四是形成工商产业投资管理新办法。完善上海工商企业投资项目备案制、核准制订管理办法，制订具体实施细则，着手建立工商投资项目网上备案、核准平台，简化手续，缩短项目前期工作时间。加大对区县、集团公司培训力度，理顺管理网络。

4. 优化产业发展政策环境

一是切实落实支持产业发展的有关政策。年初，国家出台了以增强自主创新能力为主线的60条政策和关于振兴装备制造业的若干意见（国发〔2006〕8号），上海制定了《关于落实〈国家中长期科技发展纲要若干配套政策〉的实施意见》。市有关部门将形成合力，把有关支持政策真正落实到企业，以降低企业自主创新的成本和风险。抓住浦东综合改革配套试点的机遇，积极争取国家重大政策在浦东先行先试，发挥先发效应。二是发布产业和技术创新导向。由有关部门制定和发布产业和技术创新导向，明确各行业创新的重点领域，编制上海鼓励发展自主创新技术和产品指南，设立引进吸收与创新、企业技术创新体系、重大装备自主创新、知识产权示范企业和专利新产品等专项，引导和组织企业进行攻关，提高产业的技术能级。根据"十一五"规划及《优先发展先进制造业行动方案》，提出产业投资导向及支持政策，编制《上海工业投资导向》，引导社会资金投向。三是形成推进产业发展的合力。市经委作为产业主管部门将加强产业导向、完善创新环境、建设服务平台和提供政策支持等工作。对于中央企业，支持落户上海，争取更多体现自主创新水平和国家战略的重大项目落户上海；与市属大集团，推动产业发展、技术创新与国资国企改革联动；对于民营企业和海归人才创办的科技企业，优化环境，提供服务平台，帮助其解决发展中的问题。对于中小企业，依托区县的工作网络抓好具体推进，重点协调解决共性和瓶颈问题。同时，发挥科研院所、研发机构、行业协会、中介组织在创新方面的作用。探索运用政府购买服务等方式发挥行业协会作用，支持行业协会根据自身能力与行业特点开展调查研究、品牌推广、信息服务等。

5. 推进能源资源集约利用

在节能工作方面，抓好重点用能单位、重点用能设备、重点产品单耗，提高能源管理水平。鼓励企业采用技术创新加快节能设备改造，提高运行效率。一是推动一批节能重点工程和重点项目。重点实施工业用电设备节电、能量系统优化、余热余压利用节能、燃煤工业锅炉窑炉节煤、建筑节能、空调和家用电器节电、绿色照明、分布式供能、政府机构节能、城市交通节约和替代石油等十项节能工程。二是积极促进太阳能等新能源和优质能源利用的示范试点工作。做好太阳能、绿色照明示范试点工作，通过政府采购或支持的方式，加大新能源和节能产品的推广应用。2006年将结合外高桥、邬桥粮库建设、卢湾区8号桥创意园区建设、虹口区四川北路灯光系统改造、标准化菜场建设、现代服务业集聚区建设、临港新城建设等，开展太阳能、绿色照明等节能、节电示范工程建设。三是建立促进节能的社会服务创新体系。加强能效信息传播机构能力建设，逐步建立覆盖重点用能单位和重点建筑物的能效管理信息网络，发布能源利用公报，提供节能的信息、咨询和培训。推动合同能源管理（EMC）机制的完善。同时，以节能宣传周为契机，加大资源节约与综合利用的宣传培训力度，引导全社会积极参与建设资源节约型、环境友好型城市，形成全民参与资源节约的良好社会风尚。

在推动循环经济建设方面，一是开展循环经济示范工业园区建设。推动企业开展清洁生产试点建设，2006年，重点是做好电镀行业清洁生产工作。同时，结合"第三轮环保三年行动计划"，在莘庄、宝山等有条件的工业区实施循环经济试点。二是大力开展资源综合利用。加强废纸、废玻璃、废旧金属、废旧家电等可再生利用资源的回收利用率，2006年以建设上海电子废弃物交投处置中心为重点，积极探索构建上海电子废弃物交投处置框架。重点开展高钙粉煤灰、电厂脱硫灰渣等的综合利用，鼓励企业利用余热发电。三是大力提倡绿色消费。引导和推行简易包装，支持行业协会组织制定并实施商品建议包装的行业自律规范，2006年以保健品、化妆品、食品行业为重点，控制商品过度包装。

第二章

装备制造业

　　装备制造业是一个国家工业化、现代化水平和综合国力的重要标志。经过50多年的发展，中国装备制造业取得了一系列重大成就，已经形成了门类齐全、具有相当规模和水平的装备制造业体系，成为经济发展的重要支柱产业，制造业规模目前已跃居世界第5位。但中国装备制造业整体上大而不强，素质不高，自主创新能力薄弱，国际竞争力不强，与发达国家相比还有较大差距。上海通过企业改组改造、传统产业技术改造，和产品结构优化升级等措施，逐步淘汰落后设备、技术和工艺，不断增强企业技术创新能力，积极采用高新技术和先进适用技术，使上海装备制造业跃上了一个新的台阶。"十五"期间上海装备制造业生产规模不断扩大，经济效益逐步攀升，成为上海工业经济重要的组成部分。

一、上海"十五"期间行业发展结构特点

（一）行业构成

　　上海市装备制造业由7个大类（33个中类）构成，这7个大类分别为金属制品业、通用设备制造业、专用设备制造业、交通运输制造业、电气机械、通信设备、计算机和仪器仪表；上海将重点发展清洁发电设备、输配电设备、轨道交通设备、微电子装备、重型装备、数控机床及机电一体化设备、仪表控制设备、煤液化及先进采煤设备等装备制造产业。

（二）重点行业发展情况

1. 发电设备产业保持大幅增长

　　2005年上海发电设备行业继续保持大幅增长，汽轮发电机产量首次突破2000万千瓦，达到2122万千瓦，同比增长40%，电站汽轮机、电站锅炉产量分别为2142万千瓦和67453蒸吨，同比增长93%和50%。

2. 输配电设备产业增速减慢

　　2005年上海市变压器产量较上年增长13%，而2004年的增速为48%，增速明显回落；高压开关板产量较上年下降近25%，低压开关板产量下降2%；电力电缆产量增长近17%，而2004年这一增长数字为8%。

3. 轨道交通装备产业发展潜力巨大

　　轨道交通已成为解决大中城市公共交通的首选模式，市场潜在需求巨大。"十五"期间，上海轨道交通车辆正在逐步形成产业，C型车已交付使用，A型车承接了128辆订单，目前正在抓紧A型车的自主研发。

4. 微电子装备产业规模渐成

　　"十五"期间，基本形成了以张江高科技园区为重点，以金桥出口加工区和外高桥保税区为延伸的浦东微电子产业带；中微半导体（上海）有限公司等著名企业的落户将吸引更多企业集聚。

（三）经济类型

　　外资占绝对优势。随着上海经济的快速发展和投资环境进一步优化，外资及港澳台资本进入不断，至2005年末上海装备制造业中外资及港澳台资本企业达到2074家，占总单位数的37.8%，资产4768亿元，占总资产的71%，主营业务收入为6055亿元，占总收入的79%，完成工业总产值5842亿元，占总量的约79%，从业人员达到60万人。外资及港澳台企业在上海装备制造业中占绝对优势，同时在引进新技术、新的管理模式方面也发挥着重要作用（见图2.1）。

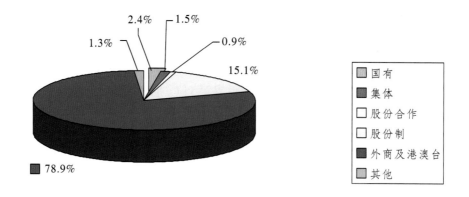

图2.1 上海装备制造业工业总产值按经济类型划分的比例

二、2005年总体运行情况

"十五"期间上海装备制造业生产规模不断扩大，经济效益逐步攀升，成为上海工业经济重要的组成部分。

1. 生产平稳快速增长

2005年上海装备制造业平稳快速增长，全年完成工业总产值7409.09亿元，比上年增长近18%；销售收入7644亿元，比上年增长近14%；产值占全市工业总产值的比重达到47%，虽较上年略有下降，但主导优势明显（见图2.2）。

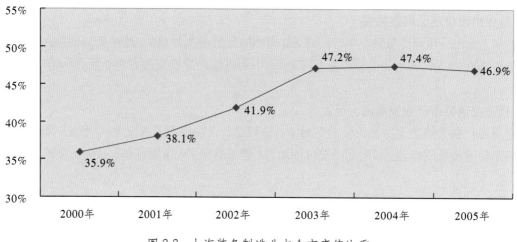

图2.2 上海装备制造业占全市产值比重

2. 经济效益有所下降

受国内汽车行业竞争激烈、经济效益滑坡、国际电子设备行业需求减弱的影响，上海装备制造业利润同比首次出现下降，2005年利润为376亿元，比上年下降15%，其中交通运输设备制造业和通信设备计算机及其他电子设备制造业利润下降显著。

3. 产销率保持高水准

2005年上海装备制造业完成销售产值7267亿元，产销率达到98%，保持较高水准，市场需求稳定增长。

4. 出口保持强劲增长

2005年上海装备制造业完成出口交货值3344亿元，比上年增长近43%，2005年出口交货值占销售产值的比重达到46%，外向度大大提高。

5. 投资增长迅速

2005年上海装备制造业完成投资额为411.95亿元，比上年增长14.2%。其中通信设备、计算机及其他电子设备制造业和交通运输设备制造业的投资比重分别是28.7%和37%，仪器仪表及文化办公用机械制造业的比重仅0.7%，投资相对集中，结构不平衡（见表2.1）。

表2.1 2005年上海装备制造业分行业投资情况表

	投资完成额，亿元	比重，%
装备制造业合计	411.95	100
金属制品业	14.81	3.6
通用设备制造业	44.96	10.9
专用设备制造业	45.88	11.7
交通运输设备制造业	152.42	37.0
电气机械制造业	32.97	8.0
通信设备、计算机制造业	118.06	28.7
仪器仪表制造业	2.85	0.7

6. 在全国保持领先地位

2005年上海装备制造业产值总量位居广东、江苏之后，居全国第三（见表2.2）；但上海在成套发电设备设计制造、汽车，船舶、中高档机床、印刷机械、大型石化设备等高端领域继续保持技术领先优势。

表2.2 2005年全国及前五位省市装备制造业工业总产值

地 区	工业总产值，亿元	占全国比重，%
全国统计	68382.14	100
广东省	13257.65	19.4
江苏省	11633.67	17.0
上海市	7409.09	10.8
山东省	6241.04	9.1
浙江省	5916.87	8.7

三、行业科技投入情况

1. 装备制造业科研能力不断增强，研发投入增长迅猛

至2005年，上海装备制造业拥有各类技术开发机构227个，科研人员近5万人；技术开发经费支出189亿元，比2000年增长近2倍，其中作为科技活动核心组成部分的研究与开发（R&D）经费支出约86亿元，比2000年增长3.3倍。

2．重点企业的研发活动情况

上海电气研发成果显著。作为上海装备制造业龙头的上海电气股份2005年科技投入占销售额的比重，首次突破4％，2005年拥有自主知识产权的产品占50％以上，占据主导地位，并创立了自主品牌；上海电气在原上海电气集团研究中心基础上组建了中央研究院，负责集团重大科研攻关项目。

3．上海机床厂有限公司"产学研"推动技术进步

上海机床厂有限公司每年科研开发经费的投入约占销售收入的5％；与上海大学、上海理工大学、西门子（中国）有限公司数控部成立了"产学研工作室"，共同致力于机床产业高端技术，特别是数控机床的研发，推动了产业技术升级。

四、2006年预测

2006年，上海装备制造业机遇与挑战并存。上海市装备制造业将继续抓住国际产业转移战略机遇，围绕科教兴市主战略，立足高端引领，以重大建设项目为依托，推进技术创新，使上海装备制造业在技术层次、规模总量、企业核心竞争力等方面得到全面提升。

第三章

电子信息产品制造业

世界制造业产业结构高度化的趋势决定了信息产业将成为支柱产业，目前发达国家信息产业产值占国内生产总值的比重已达40%～60%，新兴工业国家为20%～40%。我国电子信息产业生产规模居世界第三，地位举足轻重。2005年，对GDP的贡献率近9%，综合实力不断增强；作为上海市六个重点发展工业行业之一，上海电子信息产品制造业在"十五"期间实现了快速发展，年均增长34%，在六个重点发展工业行业中比重达40.3%，行业总体规模扩大，出口能力强，科技投入增大，技术水平提高，但也存在着行业附加值低、自主创新能力弱、成本费用上升快和竞争加剧等不利因素。

一、"十五"期间行业发展结构特点

"十五"期间，上海电子信息产品制造业实现了高速发展，2005年完成工业总产值是2000年的近4倍，年均增长34%，是"十五"期间全市工业发展最快的行业，占全市工业总产值比重从2000年的12.7%提高到25.5%。

（一）行业构成

2005年上海信息产品制造业在高增长的同时，产业结构调整加快。电子计算机制造业、通信设备制造业、集成电路制造业三个行业的工业产值占全市电子信息产品制造业工业总产值的比重达67%（见表3.1）。

表 3.1　2005年上海电子信息产品制造业情况

单位：亿元

行　　业	主营业务收入	比重 %	资产总计	比重 %	利润总额	比重 %
电子信息产品制造业	4105.95	100	2913.60	100	100.56	100
通信设备制造业	622.28	15.2	417.54	14.3	7.61	7.6
广播电视设备制造业	16.55	0.4	10.71	0.4	0.08	0.1
电子计算机制造业	1878.12	45.7	579.51	19.9	21.76	21.6
家用视听设备制造业	235.52	5.7	183.91	6.3	1.77	1.8
电子测量仪器制造业	76.18	1.9	70.18	2.4	8.91	8.9
电子专用设备制造业	80.84	2.0	89.89	3.1	6.92	6.9
电子元件制造业	380.35	9.3	381.59	13.1	31.49	31.3
电子器件制造业	479.61	11.7	914.87	31.4	-3.24	-3.2
集成电路制造业	250.05	6.1	560.13	19.2	1.13	1.1
电子机电产品制造业	311.90	7.6	244.19	8.4	20.75	20.6
电子专用材料制造业	24.60	0.6	21.21	0.7	4.51	4.5

（二）主要行业发展情况

"十五"期间电子信息产品制造业中主要行业发展良好，集成电路行业技术水平继续提高，电子计算机制造业在电子信息产品制造业中发展速度最快，此外通信设备制造业也继续保持良好增长态势。

1. 集成电路行业

集成电路发展是信息技术产业群的核心和基础，上海已成为全国规模最大、水平最高、配套最全和出口最多的集成电路制造、设计和封装中心。2005年，集成电路制造业实现主营业务收入250亿

元，比2000年增长4倍。"十五"期间上海集成电路行业逐步形成了浦东新区为主的集成电路生产线的微电子产业带，以张江、漕河泾等高科技园区为代表的集成电路设计基地，以及以松江、青浦等区域相对集中的加工制造、封装、测试基地。"十五"期间，上海集成电路行业新增31户企业，其中，规模最大的中芯国际集成电路制造（上海）有限公司一期投资超过16亿美元，是目前国内投资规模最大、技术水准最先进的芯片制造企业。拥有中国大陆第一条8英寸代工生产线的上海华虹NEC有限公司大规模集成电路的月投产量从2.5万片提高到5万片，加工工艺从0.35微米提高到0.18微米（见表3.2）。

表3.2 "十五"期间全市集成电路生产量

单位：亿块

年　份	半导体	比上年增长 %	大规模 集成电路	比上年增长 %
2001 年	22.53	-	10.7	-
2002 年	33.95	50.7	18.6	73.8
2003 年	39.73	17	21.94	18
2004 年	54.87	38.1	33.75	53.8
2005 年	67.7	23.4	38.19	13.2

2．电子计算机制造业

2005年电子计算机制造业主营业务收入达到1878亿元，比"九五"期末增长13.7倍；微型计算机产量2176万台，比"九五"期末增长51倍。世界最大的笔记本电脑生产商广达集团在松江出口加工区投资了以达丰（上海）电脑有限公司为首的"QSMC广达上海制造城"，电子计算机制造业在"十五"期间实现了飞跃式发展。

3．通信设备制造业

2005年，在全市电子信息产品制造业增幅趋缓的情况下，通信设备制造业实现主营业务收入622亿元，仍然比上年增长65%，对电子信息产品制造业增长贡献率达33%，比2000年增长1.4倍;移动通信手持机（手机）产量1939万部，比2000年增长1.9倍。

（三）经济类型

外资企业是行业的主要构成部分。信息产品制造行业是我国最早与国际接轨的产业，上海凭借地理、人才等优势吸引了大量外来资本。2000年，外商及港澳台投资企业主营业务收入占全市电子信息产品制造业比重为90%。2005年，这一比重又提高3个百分点，其中，港澳台商投资企业在"十五"期间新增较多，发展较快，占全市电子信息产品制造业比重从13%提高到25%。

二、2005年总体运行现状

1．2005年电子信息产品制造业发展快速

全年完成工业总产值4029亿元，增幅达26%，占全市工业总产值比重达25.5%，在上海工业经济中已占据极其重要的位置。（见图3.1）

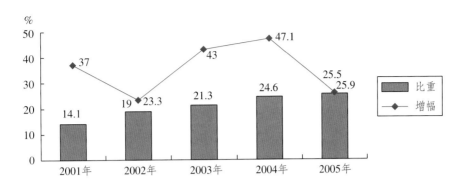

图 3.1 电子信息产品制造业工业总产值增幅和占全市工业比重

2. 出口能力增强

上海电子信息产品制造业已全面参与世界IT制造业的分工，为全市工业出口起到支撑和拉动作用。2005年全市电子信息产品制造业出口交货值2756亿元，比上年增长31%，占全市出口交货值比重55%，外向度70%以上。

3. 在全国的电子信息产业中占有重要地位

上海电子信息产品制造业主要产品在全国具有较高的市场占有率。2005年上海生产微型电子计算机2176万台，占全国产量的27%；程控交换机产量达2010万线，占29%；半导体集成电路产量67.7亿块，占25.5%，其中大规模集成电路38亿块，占近39%（见表3.3）。

表3.3 上海部分主要信息产品产量占全国比重

单位：%

产品名称	2001 年	2002 年	2003 年	2004 年	2005 年
微机	5.4	5.1	23.8	16.3	26.9
程控交换机	24.3	20.9	25.5	24.3	28.9
半导体集成电器	35.4	35.3	28.6	18.8	25.5
其中：大规模集成电路	48.1	45.0	40.9	28.1	38.9

三、行业科技投入情况

1. 全行业科技创新日趋深入

2005年，全市电子信息产品制造业技术开发经费支出70.69亿元，研发经费支出34亿元，分别比2000年增长2.3倍和2.9倍，占全市工业的26.5%和28.1%，在全市工业中科技经费投入最高。电子信息产品制造业完成新产品产值607.7亿元，新产品率15%，比上年提高6.5个百分点。

2. 重点企业科技创新情况

中芯国际集成电路制造有限公司是目前国内唯一一家能够生产12英寸芯片的企业，能够提供0.35微米到90纳米及更先进技术工艺和8英寸、12英寸芯片代工服务。公司目前拥有800多名研发人员，公司不断加大研发投入，产品向高端方向发展。

上海华虹——NEC电子有限公司2005年研发费用达1.9千万元人民币，同比增长4.6%，占销售收入的比例达14.5%，为了应对激烈的国际国内竞争，公司决定继续加大研发投入，加强自主开发、自主创新能力，同时加强知识产权保护，并加大关键设备和材料的研发。

上海贝尔阿尔卡特股份有限公司作为中国领先的全面通信解决方案供应商，产品覆盖固定语音网络、移动通信网络、数据通信网络、智能光交换网络、网络应用、系统集成与服务、多媒体终端等。

四、2006 年发展预测

2006 年上海市信息产品制造产业面临的机遇与挑战并存。全球经济平稳增长，国内发展环境日趋完善，都将为产业的发展提供良好的环境；但同时国际市场竞争进一步加剧，国际汇率波动，资源与环境约束日益增强，使电子信息产业面临新的挑战。

2006 年上海电子信息产品制造业将继续增强企业技术创新能力，推动各种形式的联合开发，争取在部分有比较优势的重点领域有所突破，争取在若干关键技术领域形成自己的知识产权、品牌优势和核心竞争力，把增强自主创新能力作为调整产业结构、转变经济增长方式的中心环节。同时发展循环经济，提高资源利用效率，大力引进外资，提高外资质量，进一步加大对国际市场的研究和开拓力度提升企业的国际竞争力。

第四章

汽车产业

2005 年国际能源、原材料价格的上升使世界汽车产业的发展环境受到影响，产能问题仍然比较严峻，世界汽车产业步入多元角逐的阶段。2005 年中国汽车市场发展总体保持稳健和理性，自主汽车品牌纷纷走出国门，在世界车坛上崭露头角，并成为世界市场新车第三销售大国。"十五"期间是上海汽车制造业的快速发展期，建立并完善了具有世界先进水平的轿车整车和零部件生产、研发体系。但由于市场影响，2005 年汽车制造业表现欠佳，各项经济指标出现回调。

一、"十五"期间行业发展结构特点

"十五"期间是上海汽车制造业的快速发展期。汽车年生产量从 2001 年的 29 万辆增长到 2005 年的近 49 万辆，累计产量超过 232 万辆。2003 年经历了井喷式发展，2004 年下半年和 2005 年呈回调状态。"十五"期间汽车产业发展结构特点如下：

（一）主要行业发展情况

汽车产业主要包括汽车整车制造、汽车零部件制造、汽车维修等。"十五"期间各行业发展情况如下：

1. 汽车整车制造业降幅最大

受国内轿车竞争加剧、价格持续走低、原材料价格大幅上涨的不利影响，在"十五"末期，上海市整车制造业企业产值出现大幅下降。2005 年完成工业总产值近 590 亿元，同比下降超过 17%，工业销售产值近 580 亿元，比上年下降达 20%（见表 4.1）。

表 4.1　2005 年上海市汽车制造业工业总产值和工业销售产值

行　业	工业总产值 亿元	增长 %	工业销售产值 亿元	增长 %
汽车制造业总计	1026.48	-8.3	1009.35	-14.0
其中：整车制造	589.96	-17.2	579.91	-20.1
零部件及配件制造	423.12	5.6	416.71	-3.1

2. 汽车零部件制造业利润空间持续萎缩

受上游汽车市场低迷及下游原材料价格上升的双重影响，汽车零部件企业利润空间不断被挤压。2005 年，尽管上海市汽车零部件及配件制造业完成工业总产值 423 亿元，同比增长近 6%；但实现利润总额 41 亿元，比上年下降约 43%；上缴税金约 17 亿元，下降 8%。

3. 汽车维修业发展迅速

"十五"期间行业产值年均增长近 13%，2005 年上海市共完成汽车维修 490 万辆次，汽车检测近 25 万辆次，维修营收 50 亿元。汽车维修市场进一步细分，除传统的单一综合性维修外，还涌现了以特约维修、汽车养护装潢为代表的快修连锁新业态。

4. 汽车零售业小幅上升

轿车进入家庭带动了汽车销售市场，涌现出上海永达汽车等一批优秀的汽车销售服务企业，提升了上海汽车制造业的社会影响力。2005 年，上海市汽车零售量 9 万辆，比上年增长近 2%，其中轿车约 8 万辆，增长 0.3%。

（二）经济类型

外资企业成为汽车制造业的中坚力量。随着近年来中国经济快速增长，国内汽车市场成为全球汽车行业发展的重要场所。在国内车市竞争本土化和长期以来我国汽车工业发展政策引导的共同作用下，世界汽车制造业巨头纷纷进入中国，德国大众、通用汽车、德尔福、伟世通、德国大陆集团等一大批世界著名的汽车及零部件生产企业入驻上海。2005年，上海汽车制造业外商及港澳台投资企业141家，占全市汽车制造业企业总数的37.2%；资产总计880.8亿元，占77.9%；全年完成主营业务收入1045.48亿元，占89.5%；完成工业总产值903.01亿元，占88%。上海汽车制造业工业总产值前30名企业中，外商及港澳台投资企业达25家，占83.3%，充分显示了外资企业雄厚的实力。国际汽车资本已经成为上海汽车制造业的主导力量。

（三）产品结构

乘用车主导，商用车发展滞后。"十五"期间，上海汽车产业围绕整车这一主线全面拓宽产品系列，乘用车车型由中级、中高级向小型、微型和高级轿车拓展，产品品种由原来四个系列几种车型增加到十多个系列数十种车型；然而，商用车的发展一直是上海汽车产业的软肋。

轿车是上海市汽车制造业的主导产品。轿车产销量分别占全市汽车产销量的99.2%和99.1%。当前，沪产轿车形成了以中级轿车为主、高级轿车和普通型轿车为辅的产品体系（见图4.1）。

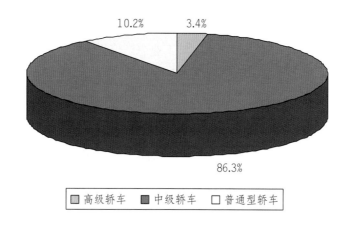

图 4.1　2005年上海轿车产量结构图

（四）投资情况

2002年国内轿车市场井喷，带动了上海汽车制造业投资的快速增长。2005年汽车制造业投资完成额81.59亿元，比2003年增长85.3%（见表4.2）。

表 4.2　2003～2005年汽车制造业投资情况

单位：亿元

年　份	汽车制造业投资完成额	整车制造业	其中：零部件及配件制造业
2003 年	44.04	19.59	24.18
2004 年	65.65	33.66	31.11
2005 年	81.59	33.23	44.87

在汽车制造业投资中，以汽车整车和汽车零部件配件为主。2005年汽车整车制造业投资完成额33.

23亿元，占汽车制造业投资完成额的40.7%；零部件及配件制造业44.97亿元，占55%。

二、2005年总体运行现状

1. 汽车制造业整体呈下滑趋势

2005年，全年完成工业总产值1026亿元，比上年下降约8%，完成工业销售产值1009亿元，下降14%，完成主营业务收入1168亿元，下降6%；实现利润总额98亿元，同比下降47%，降幅居六个重点发展工业行业之首（见表4.3）。

表4.3 2005年上海汽车制造业工业总产值和工业销售产值

行 业	工业总产值 亿元	增长 %	工业销售产值 亿元	增长 %
汽车制造业总计	1026.48	-8.3	1009.35	-14.0
其中：整车制造	589.96	-17.2	579.91	-20.1
零部件及配件制造	423.12	5.6	416.71	-3.1

近两年汽车制造业占全市工业总产值的比重呈逐年下降趋势。2005年，汽车制造业总产值仅占全市工业的6.5%，为"十五"期间最低年份（见图4.2）。

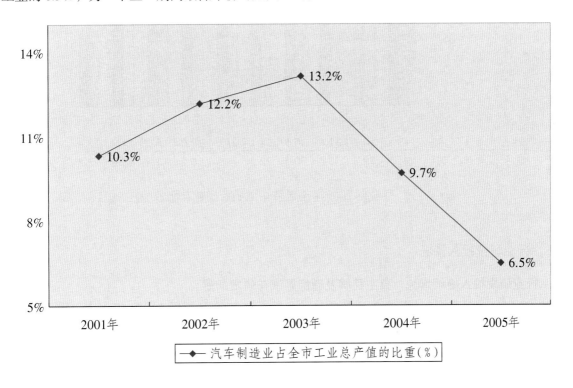

图4.2 汽车制造业占全市工业总产值的比重

2. 汽车产销连续两年负增长，轿车产销复苏迹象明显

2005年上海市全年产销均未能实现增长，连续两年出现下降。为轿车销售总体呈现先低后高的走势，上半年各月产销同比均呈两位数下降，下半年除11月份外，其余各月均同比增长，复苏迹象明显。

3. 汽车产品出口大幅增长

2005年，全年完成出口交货值94亿元，比上年增长34%。其中，整车制造业完成28亿元，增长30%；零部件及配件制造业完成65亿元，增长约36%。

4. 轿车产量占全国重要地位

2005年，上海产量为48万辆，列全国第一；广东40万辆，全国第二；其余依次是天津、吉林、北京、湖北、安徽、重庆、江苏和浙江（见图4.3）。但"十五"期间，上海轿车生产所占全国份额呈逐年下降趋势。

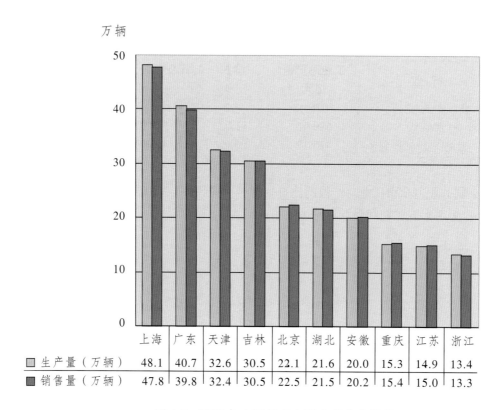

	上海	广东	天津	吉林	北京	湖北	安徽	重庆	江苏	浙江
生产量（万辆）	48.1	40.7	32.6	30.5	22.1	21.6	20.0	15.3	14.9	13.4
销售量（万辆）	47.8	39.8	32.4	30.5	22.5	21.5	20.2	15.4	15.0	13.3

图 4.3　2005年全国轿车主要生产省市排序

三、行业科技投入情况

1. 行业研发投入继续增长，自主品牌及新能源汽车研发加速

2005年底，上海市汽车制造业拥有各类技术开发机构37个，科研人员0.67万人，项目研发595项。全年技术开发经费支出66.55亿元，同比增长67.9%，其中研究与开发（R&D）经费内部支出35.02亿元，同比增长61.4%。目前，上汽集团拥有2家国家级认定的汽车技术中心和15个上海市认定的企业技术中心，并与国内著名院校建立了7个产、学、研工程中心，为开展自主品牌建设奠定了坚实基础。

2. 主要企业科技研发情况

上海大众研发成果显著。2005年主要由中方设计师完成的"PASSAT领驭"获得"中国顾客最满意的中高级轿车"称号；在混合动力项目上，上海大众计划为2008北京奥运会生产500辆混合动力轿车，并预计在2010年上海世博会前实现规模投产。

上海通用研发实力不断增强。2005年上海通用汽车共投入约13亿元资金用于新产品开发,占到总销售金额的3%左右,与公司配套的泛亚汽车工程中心在汽车外观设计、整车分析等方面都具有较强实力,目前已计划于2008年推出混合动力型中高档轿车。

上海华普努力打造自主品牌。上海华普汽车依靠自主研发,致力于打造具有海派特色的民族汽车品牌; 2005年公司研发投入占销售额的2%,计划2006年提高到5%。

四、2006年发展预测

2006年,随着轿车价格趋于稳定,消费者持币待购的现象将减少,前两年积累的需求将得到释放,加之各大城市轿车限污政策的陆续生效以及燃油税改革方案可能出台,旧车更新将加速,国内轿车市场将迎来销售小高峰。全国轿车产销继续增长,但行业实现利润仍将下降。不过市场竞争更加激烈,轿车降价虽然不可避免,但降价幅度逐步缩小,各主流车型的价格将相对均衡。车型成为市场竞争的关键,新车型的投放力度和速度都将大大超过2005年。上海新能源汽车开发力度加大。

第五章

石油化工及精细化工业

　　石油及精细化工行业既是能源工业,又是基础原材料工业,对各国各地区经济发展具有重要战略意义,从2004年开始,石化工业开始复苏,并保持着强劲的势头,在这期间美国、加拿大化工业稳步增长,投资持续升温,欧洲发展势头相对较弱;我国由于经济增长速度较快,较高需求带动了石油化工业的迅猛发展;上海市石油化工和精细化工制造业生产稳定增长,经营业绩显著,对上海工业经济增长的拉动作用日益明显,行业整体在国内处于领先地位。

一、"十五"期间行业发展结构特点

　　"十五"期间,上海市石油化工及精细化工制造业稳步增长,伴随油价上升,产品利润大幅上升;产品结构稳步调整,产品技术含量不断提高;固定资产投资力度加大,集聚优势初步体现。

1. 行业结构趋于合理,产品结构更加优化

　　"十五"期间,上海市石油化工及精细化工制造业遵循发展优势产品、淘汰劣势产品的原则,关闭了能耗高的小化肥厂;退出成本高、附加价值低的胶鞋行业、化工装备行业;搬迁重污染的染料、试剂行业。合理科学的产业链已初见端倪。

　　从产品结构看,呈现以下特点:一是油品增长较快,产品结构有所变化。二是农用化学品直线下降。三是无机化工增长放缓。四是部分有机化工原料因新建装置投产,产量增长较快。

2. 化学原料及化学制品制造业成为出口交货值增长的主力军

　　2005年,化学原料及化学制品业完成116.45亿元,占石油化工业及精细化工制造业出口交货值的比重为89%,成为带动石油及精细化工业出口交货值增长的主力军。接下来依次为化学纤维制造业、石油加工、炼焦业。

3. 化工区的建成投产,成为上海石油化工及精细化工制造业发展的新亮点

　　作为一种新型的经济发展模式,化工园区经济以其集中、集约和规模化等优势为发展注入了新的活力。2005年上海化工区完成工业总产值近150亿元,开始起步,对整个行业的贡献率达35%,成为上海工业经济发展新的增长点。

4. 循环经济建设逐步推进,初步构建起化工区发展循环经济的体系框架

　　上海化工区从招商引资开始,精心编制一条有机连接上中下游企业的一体化产业链。在这条链条上,"上一环节的产品、副产品和废物正好是下一环节的原料","上一环节的废气正好是下一环节的能源",对资源的利用达到"吃干榨尽"的程度。

5. 外资企业发展迅猛,支撑作用日益明显

　　2005年末,全市石油化工及精细化工制造业外资企业共有339户,年末资产总计近876亿元,全年实现主营业务收入1022亿元,利润总额约42亿元,分别占石油化工及精细化工制造业的38%、62%、57%和72%,对上海石油化工及精细化工制造业发展的支撑作用日益显现(见表5.1)。

表5.1　"十五"期间上海外资企业石油化工和精细化工制造业主要指标情况表

单位:亿元

年　份	单位数户	比重%	主营业务收入	比重%	利润总额	比重%	资产总计	比重%
2001年	266	32.3	439.46	55.2	13.03	51.6	559.64	59.9
2002年	216	33.2	484.03	56.9	23.98	58.6	570.30	58.8
2003年	249	35.8	621.47	56.8	34.07	62.4	623.75	59.9
2004年	286	37.4	797.06	57.7	73.81	73.7	689.40	59.8
2005年	339	38.1	1022.35	57.5	41.97	72.2	875.63	61.8

二、2005 年行业总体运行现状

1. 生产持续增长

2005 年，上海石油化工及精细化工制造业完成工业总产值 1784 亿元，比 2000 年增长近 70%；实现主营业务收入 1779 亿元，比 2000 年增长 1.2 倍，年均增长 17%。"十五"期间，石油化工及精细化工制造业工业总产值占全市的比重均在 16% 以上，进一步巩固了在全市工业经济中的重要地位（见图 5.1）。

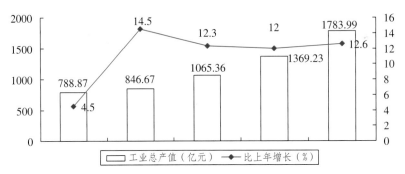

图 5.1 "十五"期间本市石油化工和精细化工制造业生产情况

2. 固定资产投资聚集度较高，产业集聚优势初步体现

"十五"期间，全市工业完成固定资产投资额近 4216 亿元，比"九五"期间增长 36%，其中化工区完成 417 亿元左右，占全市总量的近 10%，对"十五"期间工业固定资产投资额增长的贡献率为 37%，是上海工业投资增长的主要动力。上海化工区开工运行，使上海石油化工及精细化工制造业固定资产投资向园区集中，投资结构明显优化，投资项目质量普遍较高。

3. 上海石油化工和精细化工制造业整体处于领先地位

2005 年，沿海地区的辽宁、山东、江苏、上海、浙江和广东六省市的石油化工和精细化工制造业主要经济指标总量均占全国总量的近六成。从生产总量来看，江苏位居榜首，其次为山东、浙江、广东、辽宁省和上海；从利润总额来看，山东位居榜首，其次为广东、江苏、浙江、上海和辽宁（亏损）；由于各省市行业结构有所不同,盈利能力有所差异,根据销售利润率指标看,盈利能力最强的为广东,其次为山东、浙江、江苏省和上海；从企业的资产规模来看，江苏位居榜首，其次为山东、浙江、广东、上海和辽宁（见表 5.2）。

表 5.2 2005 年六省市石油化工和精细化工制造业主要经济指标表

单位：亿元

省 市	工业总产值	比重 %	主营业务收入	比重 %	利润总额	比重 %	上缴税金	比重 %	资产总计	比重 %
全国合计	24695.85	100	24581.91	100	516.38	100	1018.11	100	16948.99	100
六省市合计	15819.01	64.1	15816.23	64.3	537.31	104.1	592.05	58.2	10130.83	59.8
江苏省	3671.52	14.9	3667.99	14.9	127.43	24.7	113.26	11.1	2459.77	14.5
山东省	3302.89	13.4	3269.26	13.3	177.16	34.3	129.69	12.7	1924.31	11.4
浙江省	2610.19	10.6	2648.99	10.8	120.78	23.4	88.68	8.7	1767.76	10.4
广东省	2386.62	9.6	2332.54	9.5	137.95	26.7	120.83	11.9	1443.27	8.5
辽宁省	2063.79	8.4	2118.40	8.6	-84.14	-	71.92	7.1	1117.99	6.6
上海市	1783.99	7.2	1779.04	7.2	58.13	11.3	67.66	6.6	1417.73	8.4

三、行业科技投入情况

1．行业科技投入总量有所增长，但科技投入力度不足

2005 年，上海石油化工及精细化工制造业拥有各类技术开发机构 96 个，科研人员 0.61 万人；技术开发经费支出 13 亿元，其中作为科技活动的核心组成部分的研究与试验发展经费支出（R&D）近 5 亿元，比上年增长近 14%；拥有自主知识产权产品产值 870 亿元，自主知识产权拥有率约 49%，新产品产值率 11%，分别比全市低约 6 个和 10 个百分点。科技投入不足，减弱了对经济增长的助推作用。

2．重点企业科技投入情况

上海高桥石油化工公司研发投入直线下降。近几年，由于国际原油价格一再飙升，上海高桥石化公司出现亏损 13 亿元，这也使其研发投入直线下降；2005 年公司研发费用为 1095 万元，仅占销售收入的 0.02%，同比下降近 60%，比 2003 年下降 62%（见表 5.3）。

表 5.3　上海高桥石油化工公司科技研发投入情况

单位：万元

	上市公司	非上市公司	合计
2003 年	1468	1379	2847
2004 年	1462	1275	2737
2005 年	679	416	1095

上海华谊（集团）公司的国有和国有控股企业在"十五"期间研发投入逐年增长，合计达到 15.55 亿元。其中，2001 年为 1.96 亿元，2005 年为 2.8 亿元，2005 年为 3.03 亿元，2005 年为 3.68 亿元，2005 年为 4.08 亿元，2005 年比 2001 年增长一倍多。创建了 2 个国家级、6 个市级企业技术中心；已获国家科技进步二等奖 1 项，市科技进步奖 19 项；获国家级优秀新产品奖 12 项，市优秀新产品奖 77 项，其中 24 项获得市高新技术成果转化认定。2006 年华谊（集团）公司的国有和国有控股企业预计研发投入 4.92 亿元，主要用于煤基多联产、新材料、精细化工、生物医药四个方面的技术研究。

四、2006 年发展预测

2006 年是我国"十一五"的开局之年，也是我国入世后过渡期的最后一年，我国石油石化市场将更加开放，多元化的竞争将更趋激烈。从 2005 年 11 月份起，众多化工产品价格已经开始见顶回落，其中，化学原料及化学制品制造业的工业品出厂价格指数从 11 月份的 101.2% 开始进入下降的通道；化学纤维制造业的工业品出厂价格指数从 10 月份的 100.7% 开始进入下降的通道，这些都预示着产业周期的"拐点"可能已经出现。尤其一些大型项目的产能即将在 2006~2008 年相继释放，必将带来新一轮的产业结构调整与市场竞争。同样我们也应看到上述项目所具有的规模经济、技术先进和环保领先的鲜明特征，将为产业的良性发展打下坚实的基础。预计 2006 年，上海石油化工和精细化工制造业将继续保持平稳较快增长的态势，全年完成工业总产值 2000 亿元左右，同比增长 12% 左右。

第六章

精品钢材制造业

"十五"期间，精品钢材以其高质量、高技术含量和高附加值成为国际钢铁公司发展的热点，产量逐年攀升，产业集中度不断提高；我国钢铁业由于国内市场的巨大需求，发展迅速，但精品钢材产品尚不能满足市场需要，结构性矛盾仍然存在；上海的精品钢材制造业在资产保持基本稳定的基础上努力提高自身的生产能力和产品能级，取得了良好的经济效益，上海的精品钢材制造业产值和主营业务收入均居全国第五位，但盈利能力最强，利润总额位居全国第一。

一、"十五"期间行业发展结构特点

"十五"期间，以宝钢集团为代表的上海精品钢材基地着重进行能级提升，实施精品战略，进行了一系列调整改造，淘汰了一批落后的生产工艺和装备，高起点建设了一批精品钢材生产线，产品结构得到完善和优化，新工艺、新装备、新产品研发基地的建设取得显著成效，已成为国内最具竞争力的精品钢材生产基地。"十五"期间行业发展具有以下特点：

1. 投资保持稳定

"十五"期间，全国对钢铁的需求量大幅提高，上海的精品钢材制造业没有盲目跟风扩大企业规模，在资产保持基本稳定的基础上努力提高自身的生产能力和产品能级，取得了良好的经济效益。以宝钢集团为代表的上海精品钢材制造业基地"十五"期间总投资约400亿元，2005年全市钢铁工业固定资产投资为134亿元，资产总计为1744亿元，比2000年增长9.4%，"十五"期间年均增长1.8%。

2. 集中度大大提高

"十五"期间上海精品钢材业集中度大大提高，上海宝钢集团公司产量占全市的95%以上。上海克虏伯不锈钢有限公司（中德合资）、上海实达精密不锈钢有限公司（中美合资）、华新利华不锈钢棒线材公司（台资）、上上钢管（民企）、上重与一些船厂的铸件生产，约占5%。

3. 品种结构、产品档次不断提高

上海精品钢材制造行业产品门类涉及薄钢板、中厚钢板、普通小型中厚宽钢带、热轧薄宽钢带、冷轧薄宽钢带、中板等，与国内其他钢铁企业相比，品种结构和产品档次已都具有明显优势。"十五"期间产品档次不断提高。宝钢的汽车板生产已处于国际汽车板制造企业的先进水平；电镀锌无铬耐指纹钢板的各项性能已完全符合欧盟的环保要求，在国内率先成为绿色钢材。

4. 产业环境大大改善

"十五"期间，根据国家产业政策和上海市城市综合整治的要求，共淘汰落后炼铁包括二次化铁能力188万吨，落后炼钢能力375万吨，落后轧钢能力405万吨，各种污染物排放明显下降，厂区及周边环境发生显著变化，产业环境大大改善。

二、2005年总体运行现状

1. 行业总体情况

2005年上海精品钢材制造业生产总量在六个重点发展工业行业中居第四位，利润总额占全市工业利润近两成。在全市六个重点发展工业行业中，精品钢材制造业利润所占的比重已由2001年的第三位攀升到2005年的第一位（见图6.1），成为上海市盈利能力最强的工业行业。全年完成工业总产值1339.8亿元，比上年增长15%，占全市工业总产值的8.5%；主营业务收入1488.9亿元，增长38.7%，占9%；产销率98.8%；利润178.3亿元，增长7%，占19%；上缴税金71.9亿元，占11.9%。

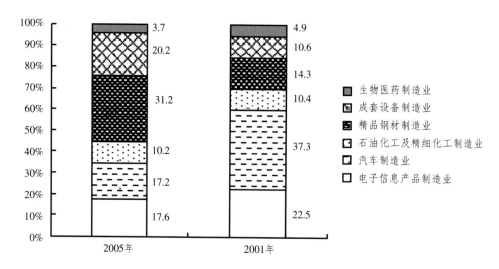

图6.1 精品钢材制造业利润在六个重点发展工业行业中的地位

上海的精品钢材制造业产值和主营业务收入均居全国第五位，但盈利能力最强，利润总额位居全国第一，主营业务收入利润率达12%，大大高出全国5%的平均水平，比其他四省平均水平高6.7个百分点。产销率在5省市中最高（见表6.1）。

表6.1 全国主要省市精品钢材制造业相关指标比较

省 市	产值 亿元	主营业务收入，亿元	比重 %	利润 亿元	比重 %	产销率 %
全国	19789.67	19958.88	100	996.42	100	98.1
河北省	3087.75	3058.87	15.3	162.22	16.3	98.1
江苏省	2922.78	2904.62	14.6	131.22	13.2	98.2
辽宁省	1666.33	1785.56	8.9	137.77	163.8	97.0
山东省	1609.53	1678.08	8.4	70.34	7.1	98.2
上海市	1339.84	1488.87	7.5	178.33	17.9	98.8

2. 重点企业情况

宝钢集团是上海钢铁工业的龙头企业，是我国目前规模最大、现代化程度最高、综合竞争力最强的钢铁企业集团，在全国乃至世界的钢铁制造业中具有举足轻重的地位，连续第二年跻身世界500强。宝钢集团在普钢、不锈钢、特钢三大领域已形成了汽车、家电、石油和管线用钢、新型建筑用钢、电工钢和特种金属材料、不锈钢和特殊钢的精品生产基地。2005年宝钢集团钢材制造业完成产值1175亿元，占全市精品钢材制造业的88%；主营业务收入1320亿元，占89%；上缴税金69亿元，占96%，产量占到全市的95%以上。

三、行业科技投入情况

1. 行业总体科技投入情况

2005年上海精品钢材制造业研究与试验开发支出为7.9亿元，比2000年增长1.8倍；实现新产品产值265.9亿元,占全市的7.8%;拥有自主知识产权的产品实现产值895.9亿元,自主知识产权拥有率达到66.9%,比全市高出12.4个百分点,在六个重点发展工业行业中位居第一。

2. 重点企业科技创新情况

"十五"期间宝钢集团通过技术创新和超前研发,拥有了一批自主知识产权和若干在世界钢铁界具有一定影响力的重大专有技术和独创技术,已初步形成核心技术链,工艺技术和生产装备达到国际先进水平,关键工艺技术开发取得显著效果,自动化和装备技术水平进一步提高,产品使用技术飞速发展,科研条件不断完善。宝钢以知识产权为主线,积极推行"技术创新里程累计制",逐步建立起以知识产权为基础的技术评价体系。2004年申请专利403件,比上年增长53%;审定技术秘密1244件,比上年增长1.3倍。宝钢技术已成功输出到国内主要大中型钢厂,以及马来西亚、法国、德国等企业。

四、2006年发展预测

2006年是"十一五"规划的开局之年,经济的快速发展将给上海精品钢材产业带来巨大发展机遇。但是由于国家采取宏观调控措施效果进一步显现,产能过剩矛盾将更加突出,且成本上升的压力依然存在,给上海精品钢材制造业带来了严峻的挑战。

第七章

战略产业

战略产业是指发展潜力较大，并对国家安全与产业安全有一定影响的产业。目前发达国家在这些行业上具有极强的实力，如造船、海洋油气开发装备、航空、航天产业等；我国虽然在整体实力上还与发达国家有一定差距，但发展十分迅速，特别是航天产业取得了重大进展，民用航空也已列入国家"十一五"规划；上海市在国内相对拥有技术上的优势，一批大企业技术实力雄厚，引领行业发展。

一、船舶产业

（一）"十五"期间行业发展结构特点

1. 造船能力急速扩大

全市造船产量由2000年的74.1万总吨发展到2005年的248万总吨，增长了2.3倍，年均增长26%（见图7.1）。

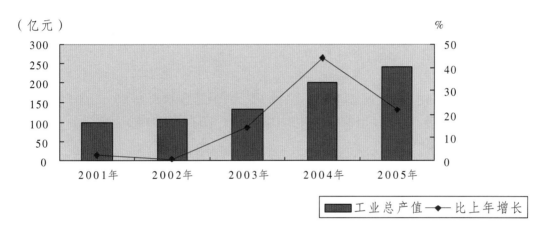

图7.1　"十五"期间上海船舶制造业生产及增长趋势

2. 主要行业构成及发展情况

金属船舶制造、船用配套设备制造和船舶修理及拆船是构成整个船舶制造业的主体，这三个行业影响着整个上海船舶制造业的发展（见图7.2）。

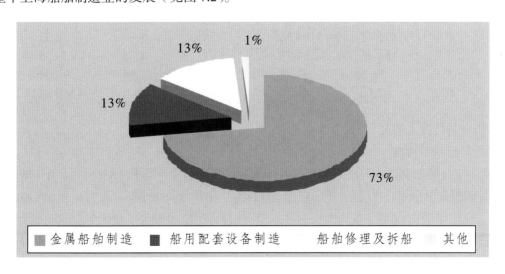

图7.2　2005年上海船舶制造业工业生产总值结构

3. 企业资产重组，行业集中度提高

"十五"期间，上海船舶企业进行了一系列有效的资产重组和资源再分配，形成了上海船舶制造业新的发展格局。由江南造船厂与求新造船厂联合重组为新的江南造船集团，沪东造船厂与中华造船厂强强联合重组为沪东中华造船（集团）有限公司，已有140余年修造船历史的上海船厂与江苏澄西船舶修造厂重组，合并组建了上船澄西船舶有限公司，外高桥造船有限公司也于2002年建成投产。2005年这四大船舶制造公司共计完成工业总产值169亿元，比上年增长20.7%，占整个上海船舶制造业的69.9%；实现利润3.6亿元，占42.6%。转制重组后的四大造船公司全面带动了整个上海船舶制造业，也代表了整个行业的发展趋势。

（二）2005年总体运行现状

1. 产销保持高速增长，经济效益取得突破

2005年，上海船舶制造业工业总产值达241.6亿元，比上年增长近20.3%；完成工业销售产值239.5亿元，比上年增长19%；2005年实现主营业务收入271.4亿元，比2004年增长39.3%；实现利润总额8.45亿元，增长2.2倍。

2. 出口增长迅速

2005年，上海船舶制造业实现出口交货值111.5亿元，比上年增长55.8%。2005年末，整个行业手持订单达855.2万总吨，比上年增长26%，其中来自国外的订单占85.5%。

3. 生产总量全国第一

2005年上海船舶制造业占全国比重高达20.8%，全国排名第一；全年实现主营业务收入271.71亿元，占24.5%，居全国首位；实现利润总额8.45亿元，位列第三。从经济总量和效益指标来看，上海船舶制造业在全国均名列前茅（见表7.1）。

表7.1 沿海主要省市部分经济指标

单位：亿元

省 市	工业总产值	主营业务收入	利润总额	税金	资产总计
上海市	241.63	271.44	8.45	4.1	435.8
江苏省	228.12	216.86	13.24	4.25	243.95
辽宁省	171.72	184.36	3.78	1.37	322.33
浙江省	154.56	130.73	8.97	4.05	129.95
山东省	96.3	85.76	4.06	1.94	94.64
广东省	92.16	84.26	3.07	1.4	140.36

（三）行业科技投入情况

1. 行业科研创新情况

2005年，上海船舶制造业科技活动人员共计达2465人，比上年增长13.9%，"十五"期间年均增长3.4%；科技经费支出达到8.7亿元，比上年增长32.4%，年均增长36.6%；研究与开发（R&D）经费支出3.6亿元，比上年增长1.6倍，年均增长51.3%。科技投入的增加带来了技术等级的明显上升，"十五"期间上海船舶制造业开发和建造了一批高技术、高附加值的液化天然气船（LNG）、化学品船、成品油轮、大型和高速集装箱船、火车渡轮等，消化吸收了LNG船、5万大功率柴油机等高技术船舶和重点配套产品技术，使得产品档次得到了提升。

2. 主要企业科研创新情况

江南造船集团有限公司是全国首批六家技术创新试点企业之一，2001 年—2004 年的 R&D 投入达 10420 万元，2005 年为 4952 万元，先后开发并建造了具有国际先进水平的散货船、集装箱船、液化气船、自卸船、成品油／化学品船、火车渡船等六大类二十多型高技术、高附加值船舶产品，出口世界二十多个国家和地区，并顺利渡过高技术产品首次商品化的创新难关，在国内造船界率先实现产品升级换代，新产品数量和技术含量均列国内同行第一，为中国船舶科技创新史增添了光辉的一页。特别是在近三年中，"江南"全面推进科技创新步伐，7 万吨自卸式散货船和"粤海铁一号"跨海火车渡船的成功建造，为"江南"在新世纪实现战略转移，加快发展奠定了坚实的技术基础。

沪东中华造船（集团）有限公司是国家级企业技术中心，"十五"期间，在船型开发和造船工艺技术上不断创新，大量采用造船新技术和新工艺，创新开发了 74500 吨和 75000 吨"中国沪东型"巴拿马型散货船，72000 吨"中国沪东型"成品油船／原油船和 110,000 吨阿芙拉型油船，自主开发的 4250 箱、5688 箱大型集装箱船和 8530 箱超大型集装箱船，始终走在我国大型集装箱船开发建造的前列，目前正在建造的我国第一艘 147，210m3 大型液化天然气（LNG）船在我国船舶工业史更是具有里程碑式的意义。在柴油机方面，公司不断推出 B&W、PC、PA 系列和苏尔寿专利技术柴油机的新产品，开发了 7S80MC 柴油机和 7RT-FLEX60C 智能型柴油机，最近又成功开发了 8S60MEC 智能型柴油机和国内首台最大缸径 7K90MC-C 柴油机。公司 2001 年—2003 年的 R&D 投入达 46213 万元，2004 年和 2005 年分别达到 28676 万元和 32825 万元，通过技术创新，公司船舶及柴油机产品结构逐步实现了由常规产品向高技术、高附加值产品的转移，在国际上赢得了较高的知名度和良好的声誉。

上海外高桥造船有限公司建立了以技术中心为核心的技术创新体系，推动技术进步和技术创新。几年来，公司共承担国家和上海市科研项目 27 个，这些项目涵盖了新技术、新船型、新工艺的预研，如造船信息技术研究，FPSO、双壳散货船、VLCC 等新船型研究，海洋工程平台项目研究，现代造船模式、关键制造技术及装备研究等，其中不少新技术、新工艺项目在公司生产经营中得到推广和应用，并发挥着显著的作用。2001 年至 2003 年，公司 R&D 投入达 13800 多万，2004 和 2005 年分别投入科研经费达 9583 万元和 19864 万元。这些科研经费主要用于各类船型开发、海洋工程开发、工法装备研究及信息化建设。

（四）2006 年发展预测

由于世界造船市场的周期演变，以及世界造船能力的总体过剩、人民币汇率调整等因素，目前船舶市场已出现"拐点"，进入下行调整期。"十一五"后期船舶市场可能出现 2～3 年的中度不景气，2008 年或 2009 年可能到达底部。但从上海造船企业的情况来看，生产任务普遍饱和，各企业船台生产任务甚至排到了 2008 年，因此未来几年上海船舶制造业能保持较为稳健的增长态势，预计 2006 年可以完成工业总产值 270 亿元。

二、海洋装备产业

（一）行业总体运行情况

上海已具备发展海洋装备产业的许多优越条件。上海海洋装备产业拥有雄厚的产业基础、完善的产业配套以及成熟的研发力量等。不仅有能够承担建造任务的上海外高桥造船有限公司、沪东中华造船集团、江南造船集团、上海神开科技公司等企业，还有中国船舶工业集团第 708 研究所、上海交通大学、同济大学等一批能够参与研发设计的科研院所。上海市和中船集团已提出将长兴岛建设打造成为世界最大造船基地的目标，为海洋油气装备的建造提供了更大的空间载体。

上海外高桥造船有限公司是中国目前造船规模最大、技术设施最先进、现代化程度最高的大型船舶总装厂。公司一直将海洋工程的开发、设计、建造列为经营战略重点，现已成功地从传统船舶行业转型为船舶与海洋工程并举的企业。2003、2004年先后建造交付了15万吨和17万吨海上浮式生产储油船（FPSO），目前正在建造中国迄今为止承接的吨位最大、造价最高、技术最新的30万吨FPSO，这标志着中国造船工业在海洋工程领域实力的突破性提升。

（二）行业科技投入情况

外高桥造船公司从建厂初期就把开发海洋工程作为重要的经营方向，抓住时机承接和开发建造FPSO等海洋工程产品。公司在海洋工程建造方面已积累了一定经验，形成了一支核心技术队伍，并建立了一套严格的符合国际标准的海洋工程建造体系和管理标准，在进一步拓展海洋工程业务方面具有高位优势和相对有利条件。

（三）2006年发展预测

2006年上海海洋油气装备产业将继续瞄准国际市场，积极跟踪、承接FPSO任务，同时推进与国外专业公司的技术合作，产、学、研结合，将目前单纯的FPSO船体设计、建造业务扩大到FPSO的总承包，大幅提高海洋工程业务的附加值和经济总量，力争使上海成为中国深海油气装备开发的创新引领基地，进而成为辐射西太平洋地区的以深海油气装备开发为特色的先进制造中心、研发中心、服务中心。

三、航空航天产业

（一）"十五"期间行业发展特点

1. 民用航空产业

上海民用航空产业在"十五"期间的发展缓慢。航空制造业不仅科研和制造资源未能得到充分运用，重大项目尚未取得转折性突破，且航空工业产品的销售量也没有得到很大提升，"十五"期间民用航空销售总额仅为9.8亿元。

2. 航天产业

"十五"期间，上海航天产业在载人航天、"风云"气象卫星、遥感卫星、运载火箭等领域为国家和上海争得了荣誉，在微小卫星技术及应用、航天机电、遥感与信息系统的开发与市场化等方面都取得了很大成绩；同时航天技术的民用开发、航天市场化和产业化已开始起步并产生了初步规模与效益。2005年9月，以研发、试制、生产航天科技产业基地在闵行莘庄工业区正式启动。

（二）2005年总体运行现状

1. 行业总体发展情况

2005年上海航空航天产业发展迅速，全年完成工业总产值17.4亿元，比2004年增长31.6%；资产总值达30.3亿元，增幅达17%；利润总额1亿元，增幅高达88.9%；产品销售收入16.4亿元，增幅达31.8%（见图1）。

2. 重点企业发展情况

上海航空工业（集团）公司是中国航空工业总公司所属的、从事民用飞机研制的大型骨干企业，在国内外拥有20余家企业。其下属的上海飞机制造厂获得了波音公司"2005年度全球最佳供应商"称号，是美国本土以外的唯一一家获奖供应商，这是国内航空制造行业转包生产企业首次获得的最高奖项。目前该厂正在积极参与我国新支线飞机项目。

上海航天局拥有几十家研究所和民品生产企业及一家上市公司，航天型号产品涉及应用卫星、运载火箭和载人飞船相关产品。2005年上海航天局在神舟六号飞船研制和发射中作出了重要贡献。

（三）行业科技投入情况

航空航天产业是知识、资金、技术密集的尖端产业，其发展与行业科技投入、技术创新有着密切联系。

1. 民用航空产业

中国航空无线电电子研究所，是国家级的从事航空电子系统总体与综合、航电核心处理与信息综合应用、航空无线电通信导航等方面技术研究和系统产品研制的专业研究所，是上海市高新技术企业，连续四届八年获上海市文明单位称号，荣获航空工业创建55周年"航空报国重大贡献单位"称号。近年来荣获省部级科技成果奖100多项，具备了新一代航空电子系统的自主研发能力。研究所拥有一个国家级科技重点实验室和四个地区级或行业级的重点实验室，具备良好的科研生产试验条件，技术手段先进。研究所坚持走"科研、生产、经营一体化"发展道路，具备航空产品多品种、小批量的科研试制和生产加工的能力。具有完善的质量保证体系，通过了GB/T19001-2000和GJB/Z9001-2001质量体系认证，并通过了软件行业国际认可的软件成熟度模型（CMM）三级认证。2005年，研究所全面完成了承担的科研生产任务，实现销售收入7.4亿元，实现收益5900万元，销售收入、收益实现了两年翻一番。人均销售收入、人均创利连续多年在中航一集团名列第一。

中国航空工业第一集团公司上海航空测控技术研究所始建于1962年，主要从事以光、机、电和计算机综合一体化的航空测控技术研究和航空机载设备、检测系统的研制。40多年来，研究所发挥综合优势，先后为航空科研生产提供了2400多项、4.2万台（套、件）的非标准测试仪器，并在航空发动机试车台通用测试系统、航空预研技术以及工业机器人、全身CT、码头及电台的计算机监控及管理系统等研制中已取得了70多项科研成果、50多项产品获得了国家、部市级的科技进步奖和优秀产品奖。2005年，全所实现工业总产值5500万元，科研生产经营总收入6000万元。

中国航空工业第一集团公司第一飞机设计研究院在上海市徐汇区龙华地区设有上海分院（原上海飞机研究所）。2005年，上海分院紧紧围绕ARJ21项目全年工作目标，及时调整计划，组织全院力量开展技术攻关及协调工作，全面展开详细设计工作。完成各类技术文件报告1300多份，发图近12万A4，优化设计预计将发出结构图纸9万多A4，系统图纸7万多A4。较好地完成了2005年的科研任务。

2. 航天产业

（1）行业科技创新情况。"十五"期间，上海航天科研取得重大突破，研制成功了高压缩比的数字图像压缩编码技术以及图像、话音复接等技术，确保了"神舟五号"、"神舟六号"航天员与地面指挥的实时图像传输及通信畅通；完全掌握了火箭发动机二次启动，大大提高了长征四号乙型运载火箭的运载能力和控制系统的可靠性；上海抓总研制的气象卫星已成为世界业务气象卫星的重要成员。

（2）重点企业科技创新情况。上海航天局现有员工2万名左右，其中包括中国工程院院士、研究员、高级工程师等各类工程技术人员6000余名。上海航天局有三项新产品被评为2005年度国家级重点新产品，这三项新产品各自拥有自主知识产权，共有1项发明专利，11项实用新型专利。

（四）2006年发展预测

2006年上海民用航空产业将继续支持中航第一集团ARJ21的研发，努力争取承担国家中长期科技规划和自主研发大型民机项目；积极发展飞机、航空发动机以及航空零部件制造，扩大转包生产，推进产业化；努力推进合资、合作项目，积极建设飞机维修、改装基地；在浦东国际机场南端至临港开发区内合理分布上海民用飞机制造业。

2006年上海航天产业在国家航天战略规划指导下，保障国家下达给上海的各项航天计划高质量地按时完成。上海航天产业除参加国家航天重点项目攻关外，还应结合民用航天应用市场的需求，配合地方与区域经济的发展，形成产业规模。

第八章

新兴产业

新兴产业以其高附加值、低能耗以及重要战略意义成为世界各国竞相发展的对象,目前美国的生物医药、日本的光电子、美国和欧洲的新能源产业技术和规模居领先地位;我国相对来说产业化程度不够,行业技术落后,尚无法对发达国家构成竞争;上海近几年投入力度加大,相对国内其他城市在技术水平上处于领先地位。生产性服务业更成为引领第三产业发展的重要力量。

一、生物医药制造业

(一)"十五"期间行业发展结构特点

"十五"期间,生物医药制造业作为上海四大新兴产业之一,在总量规划、整体布局、产业结构、运行质量等方面都进行了大幅度的调整,为行业的可持续发展打下了坚实的基础,在激烈的市场竞争中逐步形成了独特的优势和特色。"十五"期间行业发展具有以下特点:

1. 在全市工业行业中所占比重下降

"十五"期间生物医药产业业占全市的比重逐年下降,从2000年的2.7%下降到1.8%(见图8.1)。

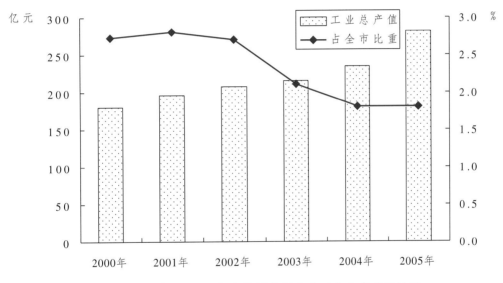

图8.1 2000年至2005年生物医药制造业工业总产值及比重

2. 产业体系逐渐完善

上海生物医药制造业体系已渐完善,涉及化学原药、制剂、中成药、生物生化制品、医疗器械、营养保健品等一系列行业。在各行业中,化学药品制造业规模最大,效益最好,2005年工业总产值达152亿元,占全部生物医药制造业的54%;医疗器械、中成药、生物制品等行业的年产值均超过25亿元;总量最小的营养保健品制造业发展速度最快,完成产值3.4亿元,比2000年增长1倍,实现利润0.6亿元;增长9.4倍。

3. 外商及港澳台投资经济占据主导地位,资产多元化趋势明显

"十五"期间,大量的外资涌入上海生物医药行业,成为上海医药行业发展的强大推动力,2005年全年完成工业总产值134亿元,占全市生物医药制造业的比重从2000年的40%上升到近487%。大量国有企业进行了公司制改革,转变为股份制企业,国有经济工业总产值的比重由2000年的近18%下降到2005年的约8%,而股份制经济的比重由27%上升到38%(见图8.2)。私营企业迅速发展,2005年末生物医药私营企业拥有资产25亿元,增长近20倍;全年完成工业总产值20亿元,增长6.2倍。

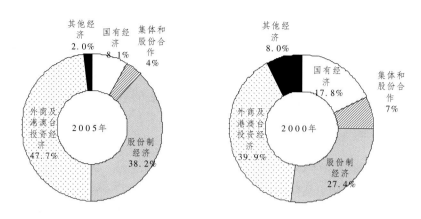

图 8.2 2005 年及 2000 年生物医药制造业工业总产值按经济类型分布情况

4. 科技产业基地迅速壮大

目前，上海生物医药产业已形成以张江国家基地为核心，南汇周康、徐汇枫林、星火开发区、青浦开发区为辐射点的产业集聚，5个区域药企占上海药企总数的55%。张江国家基地已形成研究开发—中试孵化—规模生产—营销物流的现代生物医药创新体系，2005年末园区内生物医药制造企业全年完成工业总产值42亿元，较2000年增长2.3倍，实现利润2.4亿元，较2000年增长3.8倍。

（二）2005 年总体运行现状

1. 生产总量平稳增长

2005年上海生物医药制造业产值近282亿元，比上年增长14%，至2005年末生物医药制造业企业共364户，拥有资产380亿元。

2. 经济效益缓慢增长

2005年，上海生物医药制造业企业取得了较好的经济效益，完成主营业务收入近294亿元，比上年增长近11%；实现利润21亿元，增长1.3%。

3. 出口大幅增长

2005年，上海生物医药制造业完成出口交货值共计47亿元，比上年增长44%，占销售产值的17%。外向度较高的行业有化学药品原料制造业，其出口交货值占销售产值的比重近40%，医疗器械制造业比重为38%。

4. 在全国所占比重不高

上海生物医药制造业产值占全国的比重为5%，上海位列第五，前四位分别为山东、江苏、浙江、广东；市场占有率为5.5%，上海的销售利润率为7%，两项指标均列全国第五位（见表8.1）。

表 8.1　2005 年全国主要省市生物医药业相关指标比较

指标 省 份	产值，亿元	市场占有率，%	销售利润率，%
山东省	19789.67	19958.88	8.2
江苏省	3087.75	3058.87	28.6
浙江省	2922.78	2904.62	9.0
广东省	1666.33	1785.56	16.9
上海市	1609.53	1678.08	5.6

（三）行业科技投入情况

行业科技投入增长缓慢。2005年，全市生物医药制造业完成新产品产值近47亿元，新产品产值率为16.6%，低于全市平均水平5个百分点；科技经费投入近11亿元，比2000年增长79%，R&D（研究与开发支出）投入4亿元，增长近75%，增幅均低于全市平均水平。R&D投入占主营业务收入的比重为1.4%，尽管高于全市0.7%的平均水平，但远远低于国际发达国家水平。

（四）2006年发展预测

随着全球经济的发展、世界人口总量的增长、社会老龄化程度日益提高，以及人们保健意识的不断增强，全球医药市场将持续快速扩大。中国加入WTO以后，国内医药市场更加开放，国内企业将面临更大的市场竞争压力。与此相对应的是，国内企业进入国际市场的难度依然很大，中药出口面临着一系列非关税贸易壁垒等障碍，尤其是技术壁垒，进入国际市场困难重重；关税的降低更有利于国外产品的进口，对国内中药市场形成一定的冲击。上海生物医药产业将继续强化市场推动与政府引导，发挥综合优势，加快体制创新，提升产业能级，扩大产业规模，做大做强上海生物医药产业。

二、新能源产业

新能源是指运用新技术和新材料开发利用的能源，比如太阳能、风能、海洋能等。由于煤炭、石油等常规能源资源极其有限，加上使用常规能源容易造成严重的污染，因此上海要大力发展新能源产业。

（一）2005年行业总体运行情况

1. 总体情况

截止到2005年底，上海市已建成太阳能光热应用示范点5个，完成太阳能光伏发电示范点7个，总容量200多千瓦，年发电量20万度。上海已建起18台风力发电机，位于奉贤区的风电场已经建成使用，每年可输出的风电达748万千瓦时。浦东御桥和嘉定江桥已经建立了以垃圾焚烧发电的环保电厂。

2. 重点企业情况

上海太阳能科技有限公司是国内前三大太阳能光伏电池制造商，"十五"期间太阳能产品的产值从100万元上升到近3亿元，产品远销国内外。航天机电近期在闵行获批土地150亩，将主要发展太阳能及新材料产业。

上海申能新能源投资有限公司由申能集团控股，成立于2005年7月，注册资金达2亿元人民币。公司正积极推进风能、太阳能、环保及节能等项目的开发和建设，增加绿色能源供应，改善能源结构。公司将参与风能开发，目前已在金山沿海进行风能测试。

上海交大南洋股份有限公司从2002年底开始逐步介入新能源领域，公司依托上海交大强大的科研能力，太阳能业务发展迅速，目前产品部分实现出口，并于2005年引入上海电气作为战略投资者，盈利持续增长。

（二）行业科技投入情况

太阳能光伏产业通过技术创新获得了较快发展。上海从2000年开始，每年对太阳能技术及应用均给予立项支持，通过产学研结合，培育了太阳能技术产业的发展。上海太阳能科技有限公司通过实施西藏日喀则地区无电乡通电工程42个光伏电站等十几项重大工程项目，建立了国家太阳能光伏发电产品检测中心、单晶硅电池生产线、装备制造生产线，实现批量产品出口，年销售达到10亿元人民币，公司还决定短期投资1到2亿元，以掌握光伏产业价值链的关键环节。

上海燃料电池汽车已完成"三代"样车和集成平台的开发，实现燃料电池在大巴上运行，并基本掌握燃料电池轿车的整车集成技术。预计"十一五"期间上海市政府对新能源汽车领域研发的资金投入力度将达20亿元。2005年上海华普汽车公司在研发上的投入为1亿元左右，其中混合动力的研发费用占了10%。公司已专门成立了混合动力研发部，2006年预计将投入2000万元以上。

（三）2006年发展预测

《中华人民共和国可再生能源法》于2006年1月1日起实施，上海将依据该法规制定相应的地方性法规，为新能源产业的发展进一步创造良好环境。上海将在2006年继续大力发展太阳能光伏产业，建设一系列太阳能光伏应用工程。结合江湾城、松江大学城、高科技园区、试点城镇等建设项目，建设太阳能与建筑一体化示范工程；首座1兆瓦光电示范项目将在2006年落户崇明；结合景观灯光的建设与改造，年内建成1~2个光伏发电景观灯示范点；正在实施的南汇临港新城太阳能光伏发电项目，容量达到200~250千瓦。到2006年底上海太阳能光伏发电总容量将超过400千瓦，年发电量有望达到40万度。

2006年上海将在崇明、南汇等风力资源丰富的沿海滩涂进一步建设风力发电场，在对崇明的风电场进行扩建后，年发电总量达3000万度。一个发电量为10万千瓦的海上风电场也将开建。

三、生产性服务业

由于缺乏2005年数据，本报告根据2004年经济普查结果，对上海生产性服务业的发展现状及存在的问题进行了分析：

（一）行业总体运行现状

2004年末，上海生产性服务业单位数为12.8万家，占全市第三产业的39%；从业人数186万人，占全市第三产业的40%；全年完成主营业务收入18373亿元，占全市第三产业的65%。生产性服务业已经成为引领上海第三产业发展的主要力量。

（二）"十五"期间行业发展结构特点

生产性服务业六大重点发展行业在"十五"期间的发展情况如下：

1．金融保险服务

2004年末，上海主要为企业服务的金融保险服务业共有近600家；从业人数9.2万人；资产总计35983亿元；全年完成主营业务收入1348亿元。金融保险服务是生产性服务业中资产所占比重最大的行业。金融保险服务主要包括银行业、证券业、保险业以及其他金融服务活动（见表8.2）。

表8.2　金融保险服务业的内部构成比重

单位：%

分类	单位数	从业人数	资产总计	主营业务收入
银行业	51.3	67.9	90.0	83.4
证券业	15.3	20.1	3.6	7.8
保险业	21.1	8.6	2.7	6.4
其他金融活动	12.3	3.4	3.7	2.4

商业银行是金融保险服务业的主体，其单位数占金融保险服务业的51%；从业人数占67%；资产总计占87%；外资金融机构不断壮大，2004年末，在上海的经营性外资金融机构达到113家；浦东已经成为中国的证券、期货市场中心，以及外资银行中国总部所在地。

2. 商务服务

2004 年末，上海商务服务业共有单位数 1.9 万多个，占生产性服务业的 15%；从业人数 48 万人，占 26%；全年完成主营业务收入 2074 亿元，占 11%。

上海商务服务业中，法律、会计、审计及税务服务发展很快，2004 年末上海从事此类服务的机构有 1300 多家，从业人员 2.4 万人，但其在生产性服务业中的比重很小，开展的服务层次还不高。此外，会议及展览服务业发展较快，上海的会展业已有企业 1500 多家，吸纳从业人员 1.3 万人。

3. 物流服务

2004 年末，上海物流服务业共有单位数 6.7 万个，占生产性服务业的 52%；从业人数 73 万人，占 39%；资产总计 6044 亿元，占 10%；全年完成主营业务收入 13847 亿元，占 75%。物流服务业单位数和从业人数在生产性服务业中占有相当大的比重，拥有资产最少而实现主营业务收入最多，是上海经济发展的重要产业和新的经济增长点。

4. 设计创意服务

2004 年末，上海主要为制造业服务的设计创意服务业共有单位数近 3 万个；从业人数近 34 万人；资产总计 1566 亿元；全年完成主营业务收入 873 亿元。

其中调查与咨询服务发展快、市场潜力大，2004 年末各类调查咨询机构有 1.4 万多家，占设计创意服务业的 47.7%，并已吸引了众多国内外著名咨询公司进驻；软件业发展迅速，自 2001 年以来上海软件产业已连续保持每年 50% 以上的高速增长；广告业发展较快，出现多种新兴媒体广告；创意产业集聚化进程加快，上海已有 36 家创意产业在集聚区挂牌。

5. 科技研发服务

2004 年末，上海科技研发单位数 1 万多个；从业人数 16 万人；资产总计 630 亿元；全年实现主营业务收入 215 亿元。2004 年，上海科技研发服务单位数和从业人数在生产性服务业中仅占 8% 和 8.7%；科技创新资源利用效率还有待提高。

6. 职业教育服务

2004 年末，上海各类职业教育培训服务机构共有 1600 多个；从业人数 5.7 万人。职业技能培训是职业教育服务的核心，2004 年末，上海共有职业技能培训机构 1100 多家，占职业教育服务的 68%。社会机构成为职业教育服务的主要提供者。

（三）2006 年发展预测

2006 年上海上海人力资源、科技资源和交通枢纽等方面的资源优势更加凸现，金融保险服务、科技研发服务、商务服务等特色产业加快发展。依托长三角城市密集的整体优势，增强和发挥城市服务功能。通过布局规划引导上海的生产性服务业向集聚化、专业化、高层化发展，为上海城市功能提升和先进制造业结构升级提供支撑和带动作用。

第九章

都市工业

2005 年，上海市都市型工业的工业总产值占全市工业的 13.3%，从业人员占 27.8%，上海市都市工业得到健康发展，形成了一批有实力的都市型工业园区，搭建了一批都市工业发展平台，已成为上海工业结构的重要组成部分。

一、"十五"期间行业发展结构类型

通过"十五"期间的培育和发展，上海都市型工业在产业布局合理化、培育各区县新的经济增长点、吸纳富余劳动力、加快国企改制、盘活存量资产、推动中小企业发展等诸多方面发挥了重要作用，成为新世纪上海现代工业体系中一个具有特色的重要组成部分。

（一）主要行业发展状况

上海都市型工业主要分为 7 大行业，具体有服装服饰业、食品加工制造业、包装印刷业、室内装饰用品制造业、化妆品及清洁用品制造业、工艺美术品旅游用品制造业、小型电子信息产品业。各行业"十五"期间发展情况如下：

1. 小型电子信息产品制造业快速发展

"十五"期间，上海小型电子信息产品制造业从最初低附加值、低技术含量模式，逐步探索走向科技含量高、经济效益好、资源消耗低的新型道路。2005 年小型电子信息产品制造业的主营业务收入近 269 亿元，是 2000 年的 2.4 倍，发展速度最快。

2. 服装服饰业和食品加工制造业的总量占据主导地位

2005 年末，全市都市型工业从业人员 72 万人，增幅达 30%。其中服装服饰业和食品加工制造业仍然是都市型工业发展的主力军。2005 年末，这两个行业从业人员为 37 万人，占都市型工业的比重超过51%；全年主营业务收入 953.8 亿元，比 2000 年增长 69%；实现利润总额近 38 亿元，比 2000 年增长1 倍。

3. 化妆品及清洁用品制造业实现利润保持快速发展

由于拥有自主品牌和较高附加值，化妆品及清洁用品制造业的利润总额增幅居都市型工业之首，2005 年实现利润总额近 7 亿元，比 2000 年增长 28 倍（见表 9.1）。

表 9.1 "十五"期间都市型工业主营业务收入、利润总额变化情况

行　业	主营业务收入，亿元			利润总额，亿元		
	2005 年	2000 年	比 2000 年增长，%	2005 年	2000 年	比 2000 年增长，%
合计	2182.49	1131.39	1131.39	111.97	47.10	1.4 倍
服装服饰业	455.22	288.49	288.49	19.10	13.23	44.4
食品加工制造业	498.53	276.55	276.55	18.48	5.22	2.5 倍
室内装饰用品制造业	182.86	99.72	99.72	11.73	8.56	36.9
包装印刷业	322.47	114.00	114.00	19.29	3.66	4.3 倍
化妆品及清洁用品制造业	140.26	122.69	122.69	6.64	0.22	28.6 倍
工艺美术品旅游用品制造业	314.39	150.05	150.05	11.30	6.52	73.4
小型电子信息产品制造业	268.76	79.89	79.89	25.43	9.69	1.6 倍

（二）投资情况

国有和集体经济地位下降，私营经济迅猛发展，外商及港澳台投资经济成主导力量。2005年，都市型工业中，私营经济完成工业总产值近475亿元，比2000年增长2.4倍，是各种经济类型中增长最快的，占全市私营经济工业总产值的33%；年末从业人数22万人，占都市型工业的比重为31%。国有和集体经济地位逐步降低，五年中从业人员共减少8万人，工业总产值所占比重从14%降低到3.4%。外商及港澳台投资经济占绝对主导力量，2005年完成工业总产值1492.27亿元，占都市型工业总产值的70%（见表9.2）。

表9.2　都市型工业从业人员、工业总产值变化情况

经济类型	年末从业人员，万人			工业总产值，亿元		
	2005年	比2000年净增	比重，%	2005年	比2000年增长，%	比重，%
合计	71.99	16.77	110	2109.95	1.0倍	100
国有	1.43	-3.51	2.0	30.15	-38.1	1.4
集体	2.21	-4.71	3.1	43.09	-57.8	2.0
股份合作	1.28	-1.08	1.8	24.33	-30.1	1.2
私营	22.07	14.32	30.7	474.58	2.4倍	22.5
外商及港澳台	42.47	13.85	59.0	1492.27	1.1倍	70.7
其他	2.54	-2.11	3.5	45.52	-27.4	2.2

二、2005年行业总体运行状况

上海都市型工业运行状况良好。从生产总量看，2005年，规模以上（下同）都市型工业完成工业总产值2110亿元，同比增长27.2%；出口交货值完成718亿元，同比增长24.3%；年末资产总计1859亿元，同比增长14.5%；年末从业人数达到72万人，同比增长7.8%。从经济效益看，2005年，实现主营业务收入2182亿元，同比增长22%；利润总额112亿元，税金总额72亿元，同比分别增长23.8%和33.6%（见表9.3）。

表9.3　"十五"期间都市型工业主要经济指标变化情况

单位：亿元

指标	2005年	2004年	比2004年增长%
单位数（个）	3866	3463	11.6
年末从业人员（万人）	71.99	66.77	7.8
工业总产值	2109.95	1740.98	27.2
出口交货值	717.70	577.25	24.3
年末资产总计	1858.67	1622.69	14.5
主营业务收入	2182.49	1789.61	22
利润总额	111.97	90.42	23.8
税金总额	72.26	54.09	33.6

三、2006 年发展预测

"十五"期间的发展表明，上海都市型工业在推进过程中，得到各区县、各集团和有关企业的积极响应和支持，形成"多方赢利、共同发展"的格局；上海工业"十一五"规划仍将发展都市型工业作为现代工业体系中不可或缺的部分，市政府制定的有关贴息、担保等政策，为推进都市型工业发展营造了良好的外部环境。可以预见，2006 年，都市型工业将延续"十五"期间的良好发展势头，各主要行业产值、利润将呈上升趋势。

第十章

工业能源消费状况

世界工业能耗呈不断下降趋势，据世界能源发展现状的有关资料，1980年世界工业能耗占全部能耗比重的平均水平为44.3％，到2000年已下降到37.7％，其中一些发达国家更低，例如美国为27.7％、英国为29.7％、法国为30.3％。我国经济的增长方式决定了能源消耗的不断上升，随着经济体的越做越大，"十五"期间能源危机凸显；上海市工业虽然经过"十五"产业结构的调整，能耗水平有所下降，但仍与国外差距明显。

一、"十五"期间上海工业能耗总体状况

"十五"期间能源作为支撑经济社会运转和发展的物质基础，长期维持供需平衡，成为上海工业高效运行的强大保证。

1. 工业能耗总量上升，比重不断下降

上海市的工业能耗在全市的能耗总量中所占比重仍然是最大的，2005年工业行业的综合能源消费量达到4936.4万吨标准煤，比2000年增长30.6％，年均递增5.5％；但随着产业结构调整力度不断加大，比重下降的趋势也非常明显，2000年工业行业的综合能源消费量占全市综合能源消费量的比重高达68.7％，2005年该比重已下降至61％，降低了7.7个百分点（见表10.1）。

表 10.1　工业能耗占全市能耗比重

年份	全市能耗 （万吨标准煤）	工业能耗 （万吨标准煤）	比重，％
2000 年	5499.48	3778.76	68.7
2001 年	5894.78	3931.58	66.7
2002 年	6249.34	3988.13	63.8
2003 年	6796.34	4304.81	63.3
2004 年	7405.64	4518.82	61.0
2005 年	8069.38	4936.43	61.0

2. 加工转换投入的品种结构有所化，总体效率高于全国平均水平

2005年上海市能源加工转换投入量为6580.1万吨标准煤，"十五"期间年均增长5.7％；从主要品种投入的绝对量看，煤炭、原油和天然气都呈现不同程度的增长，但从投入的比重看，煤炭比重有所下降，原油和天然气比重不断上升，2005年煤炭投入量占全市加工转换投入量的51.1％，比2000年下降5个百分点，原油、天然气投入量所占比重为42.6％和1.1％，分别比2000年上升5.3个和0.9个百分点（见图10.1）。

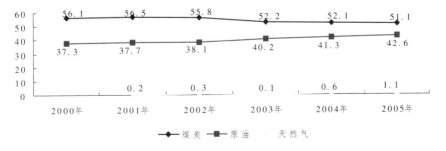

图 10.1　主要能源品种加工转换投入量所占比重（单位：％）

"十五"期间上海的能源加工转换效率高于全国平均水平。2005年上海能源加工转换总效率为75%，比"十五"期初上升0.5个百分点，比全国2004年的平均水平高出4.3个百分点。分项效率中火力发电和供热效率较为领先，2005年上海水平为42.2%，高出全国2004年平均水平2.8个百分点。

3. 能源终端消费继续上升，传统大用户的终端能耗比重有所下降

2005年全市工业行业的终端能耗达4558.09万吨标准煤，比2000年增长30%，"十五"期间年均递增5.5%，其中天然气、热力、电力终端消耗增长较快，"十五"期间年均增长分别为75.7%、25.5%和9.4%；煤炭、成品油增长较慢，年均仅增0.1%和3.9%（见图10.2）。

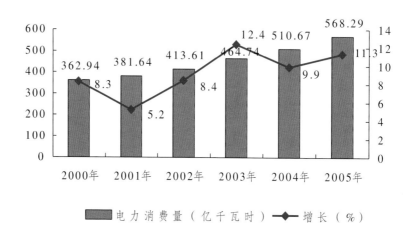

图 10.2 上海工业电力终端消费状况

上海的一些基础工业仍然是能源终端消费的大用户。2005年上海市黑色金属冶炼及压延加工业、石油加工、炼焦及核燃料加工业、化学原料及化学制品制造业、非金属矿物制造业、通用设备制造业和纺织业六个传统行业的终端能耗达3379.4万吨标准煤，占全市工业终端能耗的74.1%，然而"十五"期间上述传统行业的能耗比重有所下降，2000年上述六个行业的终端能耗比重高达78.8%，比2005高出4个百分点。

4. 单位产值能耗逐年下降，能源经济效益不断提高

"十五"期间上海规模以上工业的万元产值能耗水平呈逐年下降的良好态势。2000年规模以上工业行业万元产值能耗为0.62吨标准煤，到2005年下降至0.3吨标准煤，年均降幅达13.5%。原因主要有两个：一是部分重点耗能行业的能耗效率不断上升。二是部分产值能耗水平较低的行业工业总产值占全市规模以上工业的比重增长较快，但能耗所占比重增长相对较慢。

5. 部分工业产品单耗在国内处于领先

"十五"期间，上海主要耗能产品的能源消费量总体呈下降趋势，能源的有效利用程度不断上升，在国内处于领先水平，部分已接近甚至低于本世纪初国际先进水平。其中达到国际先进水平的有吨钢综合能耗（宝钢股份）、水泥综合能耗；此外，供电标准煤耗、乙烯综合能耗、烧碱综合能耗在国内处于领先地位（见表10.2）。

表 10.2 上海主要耗能产品能源消费量

产品能耗	计量单位	2000 年	2005 年	下降，%	目前全国平均水平	本世纪初国际先进水平
吨钢综合能耗（宝钢股份）	千克标煤 / 吨	713	687	-3.6	760	699
供电标准煤耗	克标煤 / 千瓦时	351	343	-2.3	377	320
原油加工单位能量因数能耗	千克标煤 / 吨·因数	18.96	16	-15.6	19.5	15
乙烯综合能耗	千克标煤 / 吨	1095.83	1011.62	-7.7	1050	660
烧碱综合能耗	千克标煤 / 吨	1170.00	1107.36	5.4	1503	878
水泥综合能耗	千克标煤 / 吨	165.35	105.31	-36.3	159	129
合成氨综合能耗（中型）	千克标煤 / 吨	2100.00	1971.56	-6.1	1914.29	1654.29 以下

二、存在的问题

综合分析"十五"期间上海工业能耗的总体情况，我们发现在不断取得成绩的同时，仍然存在着以下几个突出的问题：

1. 工业能耗比重仍然偏高

分析上海市各产业能耗比重可以看出，工业能耗仍然是最大部分，比重超过60%，与发达国家相比，差距明显；较高比例的工业能耗必然不不利于环境保护，不利于走可持续性的发展道路。根据《上海市国民经济和社会发展第十一个五年规划纲要》的要求，"十一五"期间上海要加快建设资源节约型、环境友好型城市，因此继续降低工业能耗的比重意义重大。

2. 能源利用效率有待进一步提高

虽然上海的单位工业总产值能耗呈逐年下降趋势，但从重点产品单耗和能源加工转换效率看，和国内领先水平，特别是和国际先进水平相比仍然存在一定差距，有待进一步提高。上海只有吨钢综合能耗（宝钢股份）和水泥综合能耗明显低于本世纪初国际先进水平，其他产品距离国际先进水平差距明显（见表2），还有部分产品的生产工艺仍停留在较低的水平能耗甚至低于国内平均水平。从能源加工转换效率分析，上海的能源加工转换效率在国内的领先优势并不明显，部分分项效率甚至低于全国平均水平，如炼焦效率和炼油效率等。

3. 可再生能源和清洁能源的使用非常有限

目前，上海工业终端消费的主要品种仍然以煤炭、成品油、热力、电力等为主，而成品油、热力、电力的生产又是主要依赖煤炭、原油这些传统的化石类燃料，对可再生能源的使用非常缺乏。2005年上海利用风能和垃圾回收的发电量分别只占全市发电量的0.03％和1.9％。

三、2006 年发展预测

"十一五"期间，随着产业结构调整力度不断加大，第三产业特别是服务性行业的规模加大，以及政府建设资源节约型、环境友好型城市政策的推动，工业能源利用效率将继续提高。预计2006年，工业能源消耗绝对量将继续上升，但消耗比重仍呈下降趋势；加工转换的品种结构进一步优化，煤炭比重继续下降，石油、天然气比重上升；能源的工业经济效益进一步上升。

附件1

2005年上海工业及技术创新大事记

1月28日，市经委、市教委、市科委联合召开上海市推进产学研合作，加强学科建设和先进制造业联动发展工作会议。会上，复旦、交大、同济等5所高校和上汽、电气、广电和华谊等8家企业集团就建立全面的战略合作伙伴关系等签署了协议。

1月29日，市经委召开工作会议。胡延照副市长指出，科教兴市主战场是先进制造业和现代服务业，要真心实意抓科教兴市，着力推进14项科教兴市重大攻关项目。

1月31日，我国第一根大型船用曲轴制造成功。这根由上海船用曲轴公司制造的大型船用曲轴将安装在威海船厂为德国建造的集装箱船的柴油机主机上。它改写了中国船用曲轴依靠进口的历史，是中国造船工业和装备制造业发展的一个新里程碑。

2月21日，市经委、市财政局和市知识产权局联合举行上海市企业知识产权工作会议暨首批上海市专利新产品颁证仪式，上海首批88项专利新产品获得市政府颁发的专利新产品证书。

2月22日，上海石化股份有限公司800万吨常减压装置打通全流程，产出合格的减压蜡油。至此，上海石化的年原油加工能力跃升至1400万吨，居国内前列，迈入世界级炼油基地行列。

3月6日，上海外高桥电厂三期工程两套1000MW超超临界发电机组供货合同在沪签订，胡延照副市长出席签字仪式。此举标志着改制一年后的上海电气集团股份有限公司在实施科教兴市主战略中迈出扎实一步。

3月22日，市经委和奉贤区联合召开"上海输配电产业战略合作推进会"，加快建立以企业为主体的"产学研"战略联盟。上海交大、上海理工、上海电力学院和上海电器科学研究所等与奉贤区签订了"产学研"合作伙伴框架协议。

3月29日，上海交通大学与广东核电集团签署了4个合作协议，内容涉及人才培养、产学研结合、员工岗前培训等领域。国家发改委副主任张国宝专门发来贺信。

4月7日，胡延照副市长到闵行区和临港产业区调研。并指出要努力发挥先发优势和基础优势，加快"提升、超越、攀登、引领"的步伐，加大创新力度，推进产学研战略合作联盟，推动科技成果产业化，提高利用外资质量，促进产业集聚和研发集聚，推动产业能级的提升。

5月26日，上海漕河泾新兴技术开发区举行创建二十周年暨跨国公司项目签约仪式。中共中央政治局委员、上海市委书记陈良宇专门作出重要批示，希望漕河泾开发区不断努力，为建设具有世界一流水准的多功能综合性产业园区作出新的贡献。

胡延照副市长、徐建国副秘书长赴华谊集团上海焦化有限公司调研煤化工、科教兴市重大项目和"十一五"规划等事宜。

5月31日，"上海华谊—复旦工业催化和功能材料研究中心"揭牌仪式在复旦大学逸夫楼举行。胡延照副市长出席揭牌仪式并为该研究中心揭牌，希望研究中心成为贯彻落实科教兴市主战略的楷模，进一步运用新技术解决经济发展的新矛盾和新问题，实现更大的发展。

6月19日，以增强自主创新能力，提高城市核心竞争力为主题的2005年上海科教兴市论坛－－汽车产业专题研讨会在上海国际会议中心举行。市政府副秘书长、市经委主任徐建国作了《加强自主品牌建设，促进汽车工业健康发展》的主题演讲。

6月21日，以加快构筑上海装备制造业高端前沿为主题的2005年上海科教兴市论坛——装备产业专题研讨会在上海国际会议中心举行。胡延照副市长在会上致辞。

6月28日，"上海市人民政府与中国石油化工集团公司进一步加强合作的协议书"签约仪式在上海举行。中共中央政治局委员、上海市委书记陈良宇，市委副书记、市长韩正，副市长胡延照，市政府副秘书长徐建国以及中石化股份公司董事长陈同海、副董事长王基铭、总裁王天普等出席签约仪式。上海市市长韩正、中石化股份公司董事长陈同海代表双方在协议书上签字。

国内首次运用熔融还原技术、采用世界上第一座年产铁水150万吨的COREX C-3000装置的浦钢搬迁罗泾工程正式全面开工。市委副书记、市长韩正发布开工令，国家发改委副主任欧新黔，市委常委、副市长周禹鹏，副市长胡延照，宝钢集团董事长谢企华，奥地利驻中国大使施魏思古特，市政府秘书长杨定华等出席开工典礼。

中国石化与英国BP合资组建的上海赛科90万吨/年乙烯工程投入运行仪式在上海化工区举行。中共中央政治局常委、国务院副总理黄菊发来贺信。中共中央政治局委员、上海市委书记陈良宇实地察看了上海赛科中央控制室和生产装置以及上海化工区部分工程项目进展情况，并宣布上海赛科90万吨乙烯工程正式投产。市委副书记、市长韩正，市人大常委会主任龚学平，市政协主席蒋以任，市委常委、市委秘书长范德官，副市长胡延照，中石化集团总经理、中石化股份董事长陈同海，中石化股份总裁王天普，英国BP集团执行副总裁亚力山大等出席仪式。

7月11日，国家科技部副部长马颂德一行视察了漕河泾开发区科技创业中心内"伽利略全球卫星导航系统"项目。

7月20日，市经委、市知识产权示范企业创建工程推进委员会领导小组召开市知识产权示范企业创建工程推进委员会第一次会议。会议原则通过第一批"上海市知识产权示范企业（培育企业）建议名单。

7月28日，胡延照副市长赴电气集团上柴股份调研，参观了上柴股份公司的411柴油机生产流水线及研发、测试等场所，要求上柴股份与客运、物流等企业优势互补形成战略联盟，开展合作。

8月3日，市经委、市国资委、市财政局、市工商局、市知识产权局、市版权局等联合召开上海市知识产权示范企业创建工程培育推进会议，标志着上海知识产权示范企业创建工程培育推进工作进入到第二阶段。

8月24日，世界500强企业之一的3M公司在漕河泾新兴技术开发区举行中国研发中心建设奠基仪式。市委常委、副市长周禹鹏出席奠基仪式。

8月26日，上汽股份与上海交大、同济大学签署深化新能源汽车项目合作协议，胡延照副市长出席签约仪式，并要求上汽股份加大产学研战略联盟的力度，突破关键技术，使上海成为新能源汽车产业基地和研发基地。

9月7日，上海电气签署了总价值近9亿元人民币的秦山核电站二期扩建工程主设备供货合同。这是上海电气继20世纪80年代为秦山核电站一期工程提供核能发电设备之后，又一次承接制造国产自主设计的大容量核电机组。

9月8日，中共中央政治局委员、上海市委书记陈良宇出席了上海电气集团党委在上海鼓风机厂有限公司召开的"深入开展先进性教育活动座谈会暨'三互动、三促进'推进会"，并作重要讲话。市委常委、常务副市长冯国勤，市委常委、市委秘书长范德官，市委常委、市委组织部部长姜斯宪以及市委组织部、市先进性教育活动领导小组和市国资委等有关负责人参加。

10月19日，市经委召开贯彻落实中央十六届五中全会精神，推进"科教兴市"主战略座谈会。胡延照副市长要求深刻领会和贯彻中央十六届五中全会精神，全面落实科学发展观和科教兴市主战略，坚持走科技创新特别是自主创新之路。

11月2日，上海电气集团所属上海重型机器厂锻造完成自重达到80吨的国内同类型最大的吊钩，吊钩的起重量为4000吨。

11月3日，随着为香港华光航业控股有限公司建造的绿色环保型17.5万吨好望角型散货轮"中华勇士号"提前4个月命名交船，上海外高桥造船有限公司今年已累计交船206.5万载重吨，成为我国第一家年交船总量突破200万载重吨的船厂，意味着我国继日本、韩国之后，成为世界上第三个拥有年造船能力200万吨大型船厂的国家。

11月8日，上海平板显示产业基地成立暨上海广电NEC液晶显示器有限公司竣工仪式隆重举行。中共中央政治局委员、上海市委书记陈良宇出席祝贺。市政协主席蒋以任，市委常委、市委秘书长范德官，市人大常委会副主任朱晓明，日本电气株式会社顾问西垣浩司等出席仪式。国务院信息办副主任陈大卫和副市长胡延照为上海平板显示产业基地成立暨上海广电NEC液晶显示器有限公司揭牌。

11月8日，我国迄今为止建造的吨位最大、造价最高、技术最新的30万吨海上浮式生产储油船（FPSO）在上海外高桥造船有限公司开工。

11月10日，商务部副部长高虎城、信息产业部电子信息产业安全调研组一行抵沪，到广电集团、华虹集团、宝信软件、展讯通信等企业进行调研，并召开座谈会。

市经委拨专款，全力支持上海医药集团三维制药公司与中科院上海有机化学研究所联合攻关"达菲"生产技术，使之尽快成为国家认可的国内磷酸奥司他韦及制剂的加工企业，以备国家储备和紧急状态下的临床需求。

11月22日，由江苏、浙江、上海三省市中小企业管理部门共同举办的"第三届'长三角'中小企业合作与发展论坛"在上海举行。上海市副市长胡延照出席会议并致辞。

12月1日，为进一步加大投资引导力度，坚持自主创新，抓住发展主题，确保全市经济持续稳定增长，市政府召开"投资促发展工作座谈会"。市委常委、常务副市长冯国勤主持会议，胡延照副市长出席会议并讲话。市政府副秘书长刘红薇、徐建国出席会议。

12月26日，中航一集团中航商用飞机公司ARJ21支线飞机客户支援中心建设奠基仪式在闵行紫竹科学园区举行。

12月30日，上海国际汽车零部件采购中心揭牌仪式和上汽工程研究院扩建项目奠基仪式在嘉定安亭举行。胡延照副市长要求上汽股份大力实施科教兴市主战略，努力提高自主创新能力，加快推进自主品牌建设，真正成为具有国际竞争力的跨国企业。

附件 2

上海工业 1990 年 ~ 2005 年主要数据一览表

单位：亿元

年份	国内生产总值	工业增加值	工业增加值 增长率，%	工业总产值	工业总产值 增长率，%	轻工业 产值	重工业 产值
1990	756.45	446.88	2.7	1642.75	4.0	846.63	796.12
1991	893.77	515.49	8.8	1947.18	14.1	976.34	970.84
1992	1114.32	636.68	17.8	2429.96	20.2	1132.75	1297.21
1993	1519.23	846.71	16.9	3327.04	20.0	1401.33	1925.71
1994	1990.86	1074.37	14.2	4255.19	18.2	1890.12	2365.06
1995	2499.43	1308.20	14.3	4547.47	17.4	2092.89	2454.57
1996	2957.55	1452.79	10.4	5126.22	15.5	2334.29	2791.73
1997	3438.79	1598.91	10.2	5649.93	14.5	2528.19	3121.74
1998	3801.09	1670.19	7.8	5763.67	7.8	2527.56	3236.11
1999	4188.73	1787.98	9.6	6213.24	10.5	2679.71	3533.53
2000	4771.17	1998.96	10.2	7022.98	13.5	2903.40	4119.59
2001	5210.12	2166.74	12.1	7806.18	16.4	2986.59	4819.59
2002	5741.03	2368.02	12.7	8730.00	14.6	3169.30	5560.70
2003	6694.23	2941.24	17.6	11708.49	31.4	3550.80	8157.68
2004	8072.83	3593.25	16.1	14595.29	20.3	3871.33	10723.97
2005	9143.95	4155.23	12.5	16876.78	13.9	4299.31	12577.48

注：1995 年以前为统计口径调整前的数据

附件 3

2005 年区县工业主要工业经济指标统计表

单位：亿元

	主营业务收入		利润总额		全部从业人员平均，人		工业总产值		出口交货值	
	总量	同比%	总量	同比%	总量	同比%	总量	同比%	总量	同比%
全市总计	16346.10	18.3	939.56	-10.8	2582373	3.8	15806 78	15.6	4972.12	28.7
浦东新区	4036.61	13.7	218.52	-21.1	462426	1.6	3763.14	8.4	1209.75	17.2
黄浦区	135.95	1.9	3.62	-15.1	21831	-12.4	113.37	2.9	16.71	20.5
卢湾区	115.54	12.8	1.77	-49.1	22838	-3.2	101.91	2.5	26.51	28.3
徐汇区	653.00	-3.9	26.81	-7.9	88708	0.5	619.89	-4.0	318.59	-6.1
长宁区	85.46	6.0	4.26	-17.1	23414	-6.1	85.76	12.3	14.13	17.3
静安区	41.81	-1.8	11.92	4.8	7756	-19.0	34.53	1.9	3.56	88.5
普陀区	188.28	0.1	11.07	-26.8	56427	-2.1	189.96	-2.5	73.62	64.1
闸北区	135.47	8.4	4.03	26.2	39598	-5.0	130.82	3.7	24.25	16.3
虹口区	75.77	-4.0	3.32	8.2	22878	-6.9	67.91	-7.3	16.49	-3.8
杨浦区	474.11	6.9	75.87	-9.1	63122	-6.1	453.56	2.8	42.30	10.6
闵行区	2212.19	27.5	116.38	-3.4	362054	8.0	2175.40	27.1	699.00	73.6
宝山区	1766.03	34.1	214.18	8.2	149859	-1.0	1609.76	22.8	229.82	18.1
嘉定区	1301.06	-0.8	67.60	-32.7	285589	5.3	1288.79	-2.5	327.10	22.1
金山区	772.07	22.1	36.70	-37.5	120295	0.9	793.56	22.6	106.92	26.1
松江区	1983.56	31.7	49.29	1.2	286845	15.0	2008.42	33.6	1372.03	37.3
青浦区	667.91	18.7	34.40	3.2	201018	10.8	687.95	17.8	226.26	31.6
南汇区	477.30	20.7	30.48	6.3	143142	6.1	478.13	18.1	118.34	32.9
奉贤区	498.92	17.2	18.16	21.1	140361	-0.6	515.84	16.8	108.65	22.2
崇明县	106.02	9.6	4.77	3.5	47363	-0.8	107.31	10.3	25.62	19.6

附件3 2005年区县工业主要工业经济指标统计表

2005年各区县行业产值及占全市行业比重统计表

单位：亿元

区县 行业分类	总产值	崇明 产值	崇明 比重%	宝山 产值	宝山 比重%	长宁 产值	长宁 比重%	奉贤 产值	奉贤 比重%	虹口 产值	虹口 比重%
总计	15806.78	107.31	0.68	1609.76	10.18	85.76	0.54	515.84	3.26	67.91	0.43
石油和天然气开采业	19.83	0.00	0.00	0.00	0.00	0.00	0.00	0.00	0.00	0.00	0.00
非金属矿采选业	0.05	0.00	0.00	0.00	0.00	0.00	0.00	0.00	0.00	0.00	0.00
农副食品加工业	150.34	0.62	0.41	1.68	1.12	0.56	0.37	7.69	5.12	0.00	0.00
食品制造业	218.25	0.17	0.08	5.97	2.73	5.88	2.69	10.19	4.67	0.40	0.18
饮料制造业	105.38	0.00	0.00	6.18	5.87	0.00	0.00	1.38	1.31	0.00	0.00
烟草制品业	199.39	0.00	0.00	0.00	0.00	0.00	0.00	0.00	0.00	0.00	0.00
纺织业	354.85	17.66	4.98	8.44	2.38	4.14	1.17	15.08	4.25	0.93	0.26
纺织服装、鞋、帽制造业	354.86	1.67	0.47	9.17	2.58	6.18	1.74	32.42	9.14	4.07	1.15
皮革、毛皮、羽毛（绒）及其制品业	109.10	0.07	0.06	12.54	11.50	0.31	0.29	14.77	13.53	2.34	2.14
木材加工及木、竹、藤、棕、草制品业	66.17	0.08	0.12	2.34	3.53	0.21	0.32	8.34	12.60	0.00	0.00
家具制造业	140.81	0.00	0.00	6.12	4.35	0.32	0.23	3.17	2.25	0.00	0.00
造纸及纸制品业	136.66	1.39	1.01	9.49	6.95	0.00	0.00	10.61	7.76	0.32	0.24
印刷业和记录媒介的复制	130.67	0.56	0.43	2.68	2.05	1.01	0.77	1.91	1.47	1.01	0.77
文教体育用品制造业	150.66	0.17	0.11	1.51	1.00	0.41	0.27	9.48	6.29	0.21	0.14
石油加工、炼焦及核燃料加工业	827.23	0.00	0.00	1.27	0.15	14.70	1.78	0.00	0.00	0.00	0.00
化学原料及化学制品制造业	1047.57	1.92	0.18	70.15	6.70	4.24	0.40	99.28	9.48	12.39	1.18
医药制造业	216.86	1.20	0.56	5.76	2.66	11.48	5.29	17.66	8.14	5.16	2.38
化学纤维制造业	48.98	0.36	0.74	0.68	1.38	2.29	4.67	2.68	5.48	0.00	0.00
橡胶制品业	143.56	1.74	1.21	1.76	1.23	1.13	0.79	4.00	2.79	0.31	0.21
塑料制品业	355.55	0.55	0.15	9.14	2.57	0.61	0.17	22.92	6.45	0.33	0.09
非金属矿物制品业	356.41	2.30	0.64	29.84	8.37	0.86	0.24	22.40	6.29	0.08	0.02

（续表）

区县 行业分类	总产值	崇明 产值	崇明 比重, %	宝山 产值	宝山 比重, %	长宁 产值	长宁 比重, %	奉贤 产值	奉贤 比重, %	虹口 产值	虹口 比重, %
黑色金属冶炼及压延加工业	1339.84	12.72	0.95	1064.81	79.47	3.40	0.25	2.93	0.22	0.00	0.00
有色金属冶炼及压延加工业	256.01	0.39	0.15	46.27	18.07	0.00	0.00	6.64	2.59	0.67	0.26
金属制品业	591.42	16.36	2.77	108.01	18.26	0.41	0.07	33.51	5.67	1.34	0.23
通用设备制造业	1229.93	13.13	1.07	69.23	5.63	5.51	0.45	45.99	3.74	2.00	0.16
专用设备制造业	395.06	1.24	0.31	19.34	4.90	3.49	0.88	15.97	4.04	13.76	3.48
交通运输设备制造业	1393.01	12.31	0.88	17.05	1.22	3.94	0.28	18.04	1.29	6.75	0.48
电气机械及器材制造业	1001.54	8.47	0.85	29.96	2.99	8.87	0.89	53.06	5.30	5.12	0.51
通信设备、计算机及其他电子设备制造业	3473.69	0.34	0.01	9.54	0.27	2.01	0.06	47.81	1.38	5.80	0.17
仪器仪表及文化、办公用机械制造业	279.88	3.20	1.14	1.35	0.48	1.69	0.60	4.08	1.46	1.96	0.70
工艺品及其他制造业	73.25	0.22	0.31	1.18	1.61	2.13	2.91	1.28	1.75	2.96	4.04
废弃资源和废旧材料回收加工业	13.64	0.25	1.83	7.60	55.76	0.00	0.00	0.13	0.95	0.00	0.00
电力、热力的生产和供应业	572.96	8.07	1.41	44.62	7.79	0.00	0.00	1.70	0.30	0.00	0.00
燃气生产和供应业	26.42	0.00	0.00	5.91	22.38	0.00	0.00	0.00	0.00	0.00	0.00
水的生产和供应业	26.97	0.15	0.56	0.16	0.60	0.00	0.00	0.70	2.61	0.00	0.00

2005年各区县行业产值及占全市行业比重统计表

单位：亿元

区县 行业分类	总产值	黄浦 产值	黄浦 比重,%	静安 产值	静安 比重,%	嘉定 产值	嘉定 比重,%	金山 产值	金山 比重,%	卢湾 产值	卢湾 比重,%
总计	15806.78	113.37	0.72	34.53	0.22	1288.79	8.15	793.56	5.02	101.91	0.64
石油和天然气开采业	19.83	0.00	0.00	19.83	100.00	0.00	0.00	0.00	0.00	0.00	0.00
非金属矿采选业	0.05	0.00	0.00	0.00	0.00	0.00	0.00	0.00	0.00	0.00	0.00
农副食品加工业	150.34	1.56	1.04	0.03	0.02	8.37	5.56	9.21	6.12	0.00	0.00
食品制造业	218.25	3.14	1.44	1.36	0.62	20.12	9.22	4.04	1.85	0.63	0.29
饮料制造业	105.38	0.67	0.64	2.17	2.06	1.78	1.69	7.04	6.68	0.00	0.00
烟草制品业	199.39	0.00	0.00	0.00	0.00	0.00	0.00	0.00	0.00	0.00	0.00
纺织业	354.85	1.27	0.36	1.27	0.36	27.68	7.80	36.82	10.38	2.85	0.80
纺织服装、鞋、帽制造业	354.86	1.98	0.56	0.78	0.22	20.91	5.89	42.70	12.03	1.79	0.50
皮革、毛皮、羽毛（绒）及其制品业	109.10	0.00	0.00	0.00	0.00	3.61	3.31	7.22	6.62	0.18	0.17
木材加工及木、竹、藤、棕、草制品业	66.17	0.00	0.00	0.00	0.00	9.98	15.08	1.22	1.85	0.00	0.00
家具制造业	140.81	0.07	0.05	0.10	0.07	16.52	11.73	1.90	1.35	0.00	0.00
造纸及纸制品业	136.66	3.54	2.59	0.26	0.20	12.90	9.44	2.08	1.52	0.00	0.00
印刷业和记录媒介的复制	130.67	0.46	0.35	0.59	0.39	6.65	5.09	0.23	0.18	0.40	0.31
文教体育用品制造业	150.66	0.05	0.03	0.08	0.01	37.78	25.07	2.56	1.70	2.00	1.33
石油加工、炼焦及核燃料加工业	827.23	0.00	0.00	0.11	0.01	3.29	0.40	422.16	51.03	0.00	0.00
化学原料及化学制品制造业	1047.57	3.91	0.37	0.00	0.00	58.03	5.54	42.70	4.08	10.33	0.99
医药制造业	216.86	10.27	4.74	0.00	0.00	5.22	2.41	7.19	3.31	0.21	0.10
化学纤维制造业	48.98	0.00	0.00	0.00	0.00	0.45	0.91	7.37	15.04	0.00	0.00
橡胶制品业	143.56	38.12	26.56	0.00	0.00	14.45	10.06	5.07	3.53	0.00	0.00
塑料制品业	355.55	1.42	0.40	0.00	0.00	45.52	12.80	24.66	6.94	0.00	0.00
非金属矿物制品业	356.41	7.39	2.07	0.00	0.00	30.33	8.51	23.94	6.72	1.40	0.39

（续表）

区　县　行业分类	总产值	黄浦		静安		嘉定		金山		卢湾	
		产值	比重，%	产值	比重，%	产值	比重，%	产值	比重，%	产值	比重，%
黑色金属冶炼及压延加工业	1339.84	0.00	0.00	0.00	0.00	25.77	1.92	14.12	1.05	0.00	0.00
有色金属冶炼及压延加工业	256.01	0.00	0.00	0.00	0.00	46.20	18.05	18.55	7.25	0.77	0.30
金属制品业	591.42	0.05	0.01	0.00	0.00	107.01	18.09	12.35	2.09	10.57	1.79
通用设备制造业	1229.93	8.66	0.70	2.97	0.24	94.62	7.69	19.96	1.62	10.81	0.88
专用设备制造业	395.06	20.85	5.28	2.01	0.51	48.31	12.23	6.65	1.68	2.22	0.56
交通运输设备制造业	1393.01	2.16	0.16	0.58	0.04	315.21	22.63	34.10	2.45	55.21	3.96
电气机械及器材制造业	1001.54	3.56	0.36	0.58	0.06	191.37	19.11	12.64	1.26	0.90	0.09
通信设备、计算机及其他电子设备制造业	3473.69	0.19	0.01	0.83	0.02	107.04	3.08	17.33	0.50	0.49	0.01
仪器仪表及文化、办公用机械制造业	279.88	0.00	0.00	0.71	0.25	22.16	7.92	3.32	1.19	0.91	0.32
工艺品及其他制造业	73.25	3.98	5.43	0.26	0.36	5.02	6.86	5.56	7.60	0.23	0.31
废弃资源和废旧材料回收加工业	13.64	0.00	0.00	0.00	0.00	0.14	1.05	0.37	2.72	0.00	0.00
电力、热力的生产和供应业	572.96	0.06	0.01	0.00	0.00	0.00	0.00	0.00	0.00	0.00	0.00
燃气生产和供应业	26.42	0.00	0.00	0.00	0.00	0.29	1.09	0.00	0.00	0.00	0.00
水的生产和供应业	26.97	0.00	0.00	0.02	0.08	2.07	7.69	0.50	1.85	0.00	0.00

附 件 3 2005 年区县工业主要工业经济指标统计表

2005 年各区县行业产值及占全市行业比重统计表

单位：亿元

区县 行业分类	总产值	闵行 产值	闵行 比重,%	南汇 产值	南汇 比重,%	浦东 产值	浦东 比重,%	普陀 产值	普陀 比重,%	青浦 产值	青浦 比重,%
总计	15806.78	2175.40	13.76	478.13	3.02	3763.14	23.81	189.96	1.20	687.95	4.35
石油和天然气开采业	19.83	0.00	0.00	0.00	0.00	0.00	0.00	0.00	0.00	0.00	0.00
非金属矿采选业	0.05	0.00	0.00	0.00	0.00	0.00	0.00	0.00	0.00	0.00	0.00
农副食品加工业	150.34	15.93	10.59	5.47	3.64	47.58	31.65	1.82	1.21	2.61	1.74
食品制造业	218.25	62.09	28.45	3.06	1.40	25.53	11.70	2.10	0.96	20.87	9.56
饮料制造业	105.38	58.21	55.24	1.38	1.31	18.52	17.58	0.00	0.00	0.56	0.53
烟草制品业	199.39	0.00	0.00	0.00	0.00	1.62	0.81	0.00	0.00	0.00	0.00
纺织业	354.85	41.53	11.70	23.86	6.72	50.94	14.36	1.82	0.51	46.18	13.01
纺织服装、鞋、帽制造业	354.86	72.54	20.44	34.10	9.61	47.05	13.26	3.58	1.01	29.94	8.44
皮革、毛皮（绒）及其制品业	109.10	14.51	13.30	4.92	4.51	6.57	6.02	0.33	0.30	18.99	17.40
木材加工及木、竹、藤、棕、草制品业	66.17	6.85	10.36	2.27	3.42	5.13	7.75	0.60	0.91	19.37	29.27
家具制造业	140.81	20.07	14.25	43.06	30.58	8.30	5.90	7.90	5.61	24.99	17.75
造纸及纸制品业	136.66	15.28	11.18	21.01	15.37	22.06	16.14	3.99	2.92	11.09	8.12
印刷业和记录媒介的复制	130.67	20.97	16.05	5.82	4.46	30.80	23.57	16.89	12.93	9.11	6.97
文教体育用品制造业	150.66	30.29	20.11	7.06	4.68	17.01	11.29	1.95	1.30	24.17	16.04
石油加工、炼焦及核燃料加工业	827.23	43.14	5.22	1.38	0.17	339.17	41.00	0.00	0.00	0.43	0.05
化学原料及化学制品制造业	1047.57	181.55	17.33	33.42	3.19	207.10	19.77	29.30	2.80	42.83	4.09
医药制造业	216.86	37.51	17.29	12.33	5.68	77.08	35.54	10.25	4.73	5.08	2.34
化学纤维制造业	48.98	5.22	10.66	1.29	2.63	0.77	1.57	0.10	0.21	18.18	37.13
橡胶制品业	143.56	10.09	7.02	6.12	4.26	20.36	14.18	1.05	0.73	10.11	7.04
塑料制品业	355.55	68.06	19.14	22.93	6.45	76.28	21.45	3.35	0.94	31.21	8.78
非金属矿物制品业	356.41	55.21	15.49	29.14	8.17	48.83	13.70	2.97	0.83	31.25	8.77

（续表）

行业分类	总产值	闵行 产值	闵行 比重, %	南汇 产值	南汇 比重, %	浦东 产值	浦东 比重, %	普陀 产值	普陀 比重, %	青浦 产值	青浦 比重, %
黑色金属冶炼及压延加工业	1339.84	10.32	0.77	4.65	0.35	147.49	11.01	0.00	0.00	6.41	0.48
有色金属冶炼及压延加工业	256.01	29.31	11.45	22.17	8.66	30.63	11.96	2.00	0.78	23.95	9.36
金属制品业	591.42	60.31	10.20	31.73	5.36	79.09	13.37	11.12	1.88	43.11	7.29
通用设备制造业	1229.93	292.22	23.76	30.22	2.46	309.11	25.13	16.19	1.32	70.15	5.70
专用设备制造业	395.06	69.69	17.64	10.73	2.72	77.19	19.54	15.42	3.90	20.80	5.27
交通运输设备制造业	1393.01	42.72	3.07	37.54	2.69	658.92	47.30	8.40	0.60	76.76	5.51
电气机械及器材制造业	1001.54	205.26	20.49	69.08	6.90	175.85	17.56	35.75	3.57	47.67	4.76
通信设备、计算机及其他电子设备制造业	3473.69	602.45	17.34	8.18	0.24	1042.06	30.00	8.44	0.24	42.74	1.23
仪器仪表及文化、办公用机械制造业	279.88	45.66	16.32	0.57	0.20	110.99	39.66	3.31	1.18	2.18	0.78
工艺品及其他制造业	73.25	14.46	19.74	3.39	4.63	4.95	6.76	0.29	0.40	3.88	5.30
废弃资源和废旧材料回收加工业	13.64	0.93	6.79	0.48	3.50	1.19	8.70	0.36	2.67	2.11	15.48
电力、热力的生产和供应业	572.96	42.80	7.47	0.00	0.00	63.95	11.16	0.67	0.12	0.39	0.07
燃气生产和供应业	26.42	0.00	0.00	0.00	0.00	9.83	37.19	0.00	0.00	0.00	0.00
水的生产和供应业	26.97	0.19	0.71	0.78	2.89	1.21	4.48	0.00	0.00	0.83	3.09

附件3 2005年区县工业主要工业经济指标统计表

2005年各区县行业产值及占全市行业比重统计表

单位：亿元

区县 行业分类	总产值	松江 产值	松江 比重，%	徐汇 产值	徐汇 比重，%	杨浦 产值	杨浦 比重，%	闸北 产值	闸北 比重，%
总计	15806.78	2008.42	12.71	619.89	3.92	453.56	2.87	130.82	0.83
石油和天然气开采业	19.83	0.00	0.00	0.00	0.00	0.00	0.00	0.00	0.00
非金属矿采选业	0.05	0.00	0.00	0.00	0.00	0.00	0.00	0.00	0.00
农副食品加工业	150.34	24.34	16.19	18.38	12.23	2.68	1.78	1.81	1.21
食品制造业	218.25	23.54	10.78	21.79	9.98	5.17	2.37	2.05	0.94
饮料制造业	105.38	4.35	4.13	0.14	0.13	2.73	2.59	0.26	0.25
烟草制品业	199.39	0.00	0.00	0.00	0.00	197.77	99.19	0.00	0.00
纺织业	354.85	38.88	10.96	1.44	0.41	30.16	8.50	3.91	1.10
纺织服装、鞋、帽制造业	354.86	36.75	10.36	4.14	1.17	3.83	1.08	0.56	0.16
皮革、毛皮、羽毛（绒）及其制品业	109.10	19.88	18.22	0.61	0.56	1.55	1.42	0.71	0.65
木材加工及木、竹、藤、棕、草制品业	66.17	3.57	5.40	4.69	7.09	0.67	1.01	0.84	1.27
家具制造业	140.81	5.79	4.11	1.42	1.01	0.17	0.12	1.02	0.73
造纸及纸制品业	136.66	17.46	12.78	3.51	2.57	1.21	0.88	0.60	0.44
印刷业和记录媒介的复制	130.67	10.54	8.07	6.53	5.00	6.11	4.67	8.72	6.67
文教体育用品制造业	150.66	11.77	7.81	2.02	1.34	0.89	0.59	0.36	0.24
石油加工、炼焦及核燃料加工业	827.23	1.01	0.12	0.60	0.07	0.00	0.00	0.00	0.00
化学原料及化学制品制造业	1047.57	56.25	5.37	41.46	3.96	5.69	0.54	3.76	0.36
医药制造业	216.86	3.53	1.63	6.10	2.81	0.48	0.22	0.35	0.16
化学纤维制造业	48.98	9.23	18.84	0.00	0.00	0.27	0.55	0.10	0.20
橡胶制品业	143.56	27.01	18.81	0.00	0.00	1.49	1.03	0.77	0.53
塑料制品业	355.55	42.11	11.84	2.02	0.57	4.44	1.25	0.00	0.00
非金属矿物制品业	356.41	42.05	11.80	12.04	3.38	9.47	2.66	4.86	1.36

附 件 3 2005年区县工业主要工业经济指标统计表

（续表）

区 县 行业分类	总产值	松江		徐汇		杨浦		闸北	
		产值	比重,%	产值	比重,%	产值	比重,%	产值	比重,%
黑色金属冶炼及压延加工业	1339.84	14.62	1.09	2.08	0.16	28.00	2.09	0.00	0.00
有色金属冶炼及压延加工业	256.01	23.87	9.32	1.09	0.43	3.03	1.18	0.46	0.18
金属制品业	591.42	59.16	10.00	1.71	0.29	9.71	1.64	5.45	0.92
通用设备制造业	1229.93	110.42	8.98	16.31	1.33	75.57	6.14	36.88	3.00
专用设备制造业	395.06	30.91	7.82	11.39	2.88	15.38	3.89	9.71	2.46
交通运输设备制造业	1393.01	44.28	3.18	31.80	2.28	17.23	1.24	9.97	0.72
电气机械及器材制造业	1001.54	107.58	10.74	18.52	1.85	8.50	0.85	18.81	1.88
通信设备、计算机及其他电子设备制造业	3473.69	1190.98	34.29	362.32	10.43	9.43	0.27	15.72	0.45
仪器仪表及文化、办公用机械制造业	279.88	42.15	15.06	29.36	10.49	3.24	1.16	3.04	1.09
工艺品及其他制造业	73.25	4.67	6.37	18.40	25.12	0.27	0.37	0.09	0.12
废弃资源和废旧材料回收加工业	13.64	0.08	0.56	0.00	0.00	0.00	0.00	0.00	0.00
电力、热力的生产和供应业	572.96	0.00	0.00	0.00	0.00	8.44	1.47	0.00	0.00
燃气生产和供应业	26.42	0.00	0.00	0.00	0.00	0.00	0.00	0.00	0.00
水的生产和供应业	26.97	1.66	6.16	0.00	0.00	0.00	0.00	0.00	0.00

（注：数据为工业规模以上企业快报数）

Part I

General

In the 10th Five-Year Plan period, under the guidance of series of principles and policies of the Central Government and the State Council and under the correct leading of Municipal Committee and Municipal Government, Shanghai industry keep economic development rapid, harmonious, and stable, play an important role in keeping shanghai economy increasing at double-digit rates for 14 years and establish a base in making further progress in the 11th Five-Year.

I. Retrospect of Shanghai industrial development

(1) Retrospect of Shanghai industrial development in the 10th Five-Year Plan period.

In the 10th Five-Year Plan period, Shanghai industry conscientiously act the scientific concept of development, carry out the strategy of prospering our country through science & education and prospering city through science & education, stick to take a new road to industrialization, intensify innovation, upgrade class, develop equipment, and construct the infrastructure. As a result, the planned economical indexes for the 10th Five-Year Plan are completed successfully and obvious achievements are got.

1.The role of industrial support and drive is enhancing

In the 10th Five-Year Plan period Shanghai industry demonstrated a rapid development trend,played an important role in shanghai economy. Total industrial output value in past five years was up by RMB 1000 billion, with the annual average increment of 18.9% in the 10th Five-Year Plan period. Total industrial output value made in 2005 was RMB 1687.678 billion in which the total output value made by industries above scale (the same below) was RMB 1580.678 billion, with an increment 1.4 times as much as 2000 The added value of industries increased twice in past five years with average annual increment of 15.4% (Fig. 1) and the average contribution rate to city's economic increase was up to 53.2% that played a significant role in prospering economy.

Fig. 1 Total output value and growth rate of Shanghai·industry in the 10th Five-Year Plan period

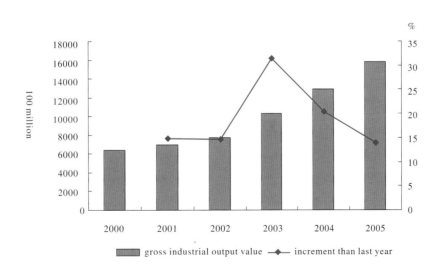

2. The role of Innovation- Driven has highlighted

Before 21 century, shanghai economy continuously increasing depends on invest-driven, annual total industrial invest accounts for one-third of the total invest of fixed assets. With the transform of economy development mode, innovation is playing a significant role in industrial development. In the 10th Five-Year Plan period, the scientific R&D increased twice, taking up of GDP from 1.69% to 2.34%, among which the enterprise R&D takes up of 62% of the total R&D. Today the R&D invest in most developed countries is generally above 2%, shanghai has taken the lead in entering the threshold of innovation-driven, with exceeding 2% in R&D invest. In the 10th Five-Year Plan period, the R&D funds steadily increased at the quickest speed and the annual growth rate of R&D funds was up to 29.9%. In 2005, the R&D funds of industrial entrepreneurs above scale put was added up to RMB 12.083 billion with annual average growth rate of 29.9%, up by 2.7 times comparing with 2000, in which large- and medium-sized enterprises put the R&D funds up to RMB 10.843 billion with annual average growth rate of 28. 5%, up by 2.5 times. The rapid increase of the R&D funds input transformed social R&D funds structure positively and resulted in that the R&D funds of Shanghai industrial enterprises above scale took up of 56.6% of the city general value in 2005, up by 13.8% comparing with 2000. The input of R&D funds was being shifted into Hi-Tech industry and the six major developing industries, in 2005, the R&D funds of Shanghai hi-tech industry was accumulated up to RMB 3.832 billion with annual average increase of 24.5%, up by two times comparing with 2000, and the R&D funds for six industrial major developing industries is up to RMB 10.483 billions with annual average increase of 30.1%, up by 2.7 times, which takes up of 86.8% of city's industrial R&D funds, from view of general value, the three prior industries and the occupying rate are respectively car manufacture 33.9%, information product manufacture industry 32.4%, and complete set manufacture industry 17.7%. Among R&D funds of the six major industrial developing industries, from the view of growth speed, comparing with 2000, in 2005 in the three prior industries car manufacture was 4.9 times, complete set manufacture industry was 3.3 times, and information product manufacture industry was 2.5 times(Table. 1).

Table. 1 The R&D funds and ratio of city's six industrial major developing industries.

Industry	2000year		2005year	
	R&D funds (RMB 100 million)	Rate (%)	R&D funds (RMB 100 million)	Rate (%)
Total	28.11	100	104.83	100
Information product manufacture industry	9.73	34.6	33.95	32.4
Car manufacture	5.99	21.3	35.58	33.9
Petrochemical and refined chemical industry	2.85	10.1	4.81	4.6
Refined steel industry	2.84	10.1	7.89	7.5
Complete set manufacture industry	4.35	15.5	18.51	17.7
Medicine manufacture industry	2.35	8.4	4.09	3.9

The number of state-certified enterprise technology center and city-certified enterprise technology center increases from 23 and 57 by the end of the 9th Five-Year Plan period to 29 and 160 in 2005,respectively. Among the more than 1000 industrial enterprises above scale, in 189 enterprise technology center above city-level employed staff, products sale, and profits take up of 21.10%, 35.3%, 79. 8% respectively; in view of the city research and test development funds, patent application, and invention patent application take up of 49.5%, 19.1%, and

34.3% respectively; development institutes established cooperatively with universities and other outer units, and the cooperating funds output of year's production, study, and research are 193, 42, and RMB2.574 billion respectively. By the end of 2005, there are 170 foreign-funded R&D centers in Shanghai. Ciba Specialty Chemicals, CISCO, Saint-Gobain and other companies have transferred their global R&D centers into Shanghai. Shanghai industrial enterprises have doublely improved their energy and power of self-innovation.

Shanghai industrial innovation production continually appeared and enterprise development mode was being shifted from Introduction-Driven Model to Innovation- Driven Model. The market-oriented self-innovation layout has preliminary formed. In the 10th Five-Year Plan shanghai industrial enterprise product innovation and technology art innovation level has been largely increased and self-innovation output capacity has been strengthened gradually. In view of new product output, in 2005 new product output value of industrial enterprise above scale was up to RMB340.876 billions, 2.4 times as much as 2000 with average annual increase of 19.4%, taking up of 21.6% of gross industrial output value; new product sale income was up to RMB 342.968 billion, 2.4 times as much as 2000 with annual average increase of 19.6%, taking up of 21.0% of gross industrial output value. In 2005 the number of patent application by industrial enterprises was 23,000, accounting for 69.9% of the total patent application in the city, which was near to twice as much as 2000; the number of patent licensing by industrial enterprises was 8,486, accounting for 67.3% of the total patent licensing in the city, which was three times as much as 2000. With the constant expansion of Shanghai industrial self-innovation input scale and the constant strengthening of innovation Capacity, in view of the rate between the introduced foreign technology funds output and R&D funds output which was used as index to weigh the reliance on foreign technology and has decreased from 1.20:1 in 2000 to 0.38:1.The intensivism degree of industrial development continuously increases, the energy consumption of industrial added value of RMB 10 thousand decreases year by year, the potential of industrial development gradually improves.

3. Industrial strcture upgrades obviously

In the 10th Five-Year Plan period, shanghai industry seized the opportunities of international industrial shift and quickened the tempo of industrial structure upgrading, the ratio of six main backbone industries output value to the total industrial output value increased from 48.6% in the end of the 9th Five-Year Plan period to 63.4% in the 10th Five-Year Plan period.High-tech industries improving rapidly,have come into being a certain scale and gradually become to the main industries of shanghai industries, the ratio of high-tech industries output value to the total industrial output value increased year by year, from 20.6% in the end of 2000 to 28.2% in 2004. Electronics & information industry has become to the first main backbone industry, with annual increment of 34%, taking up of 25.5% of gross industrial output value, played a significant role in prospering the industrial output. The foundational industries such as petrol chemistry and iron & steel industry step up the industry structure adjustment and updating, gradually carry out the amalgamation with high-tech industries.The proportion between light industry and heavy industry basically keeps stable in the level of 3:7, tallying to the middle and late phase character of international typical heavy industrialition,shows that shanghai industries are in a continuously steady increase phase of heavy industrialition, shanghai industrial structue walking up to high-level development direction.

4. Constantly optimize industrial investment structure

In the 10th Five-Year Plan shanghai gross industrial investment was about RMB450 billion, and annual investment kept 1/3 of the social fixed investment, structure was likely to reasonable, and industrial investment concentrated on and major industry base furthermore. In the 10th Five–Year Plan, six major industries gross investment climbed to about RMB 260 billion, accounting for 61% of the gross industrial investment; foreign investment accounts for 28% of the city industrial investment, and private investment accounts for 15% of industrial investment; in addition, by implementing the strategy of going out and serving the nation, in the 10th Five–Year Plan, the city industrial foreign investment increases constantly and has climbed up to RMB 20 billion, accounting for 5% of the local investment, conducting shanghai–made products to enter into the international market. As a result in the 10th Five–Year Plan Whole city industry extroversion (export delivery value accounts for gross industrial output value proportion) was enhanced unceasingly, and climbed to 31.5%, up by 11% over 2000.

5.The readjustment of industrial layout was successful obviously

In the 10th Five–Year Plan, shanghai adjusted industry layout in a large range furthermore,centered on the suburb shanghai enterprises layout shifted industrial emphasis to suburb and focused industries on Industry Park.

First is to speed up industry base and development construction. Except consolidating refined steel industry base auto, Petrochemical, and microelectronic industry base construction are raised to highlight to develop. Meanwhile establish the strategy of building development zone above city level with proper priority. Second is to liquidize old industry factory remnant assets in central city, endeavor to construct metropolis industry garden zones and idea–creation industry concentration zones, and actively develop employment, environment protection metropolis industry with combination of the change of city function. By the end of 2005 totally as many as 230 metropolis industry garden zones (buildings) and 30 idea–creation industry concentration zones are set up, more than 4 million sqm old industry factories are liquidized, and 700 thousand people are employed. Third is to form industry concentration group based on industry chain by pushing industry park to focus on garden zones. According to estimate, six major industry bases and industries in industry park zones above city level have possessed 50% of the concentration. In the late 10th Five–Year Plan the adjustment of development zone has helped to increase national industrial zone to 5 (Waigaoqiao Free Trade Zone, Jinqiao Export Processing Zone, Zhangjiang High–tech Park, Caohejing High–tech Park, and Minhang economic technical developing area) and city development zone to 13.

(II)The main characteristic of Shanghai industrial development in 2005

1. The continual gr owth of industry scale gross

The whole city's industry production kept the stable growth. The industry overall production value reached to RMB1580.678 billion, a rise of 13.9%, than last year. The industry Enterprise reached 14,800 thousand, the overall asset reached to RMB1589.344 billion, the employment reached to RMB 2.5824 million, the main operation income finished in full year was RMB1634.61 billion.

(1) from the view of subjection, the overall production value realized by district and county industry occupied 58%,the central industry occupied 21.8%,the main area industry (11 group cooperation belonging to city such as: electric, automobile, Huayi、broadcast electricity, instrument electricity, light industry, textile,building material, colored, computer)occupied 17.4% (referring to table 2)

(2) From the view of main industry: The overall production value realized by electricity, machinery industry occupied 22% and 19.8% respectively. The total of light industry, petrol chemistry, metallurgy, automobile occupied 43.4%, the other industry occupied 24.8% (referring to table 3).

Table 2 The completion situation of main economy index about subjection relation in 2005 year.

Unit: RMB billion

Index	Type	Above scale	Central industry	Main place	District and county industry	Other
Asset gross	quantity	15893.4	4557.3	3141	7311.5	883.6
	proportion	-	28.7%	19.8%	46%	5.6%
Total production value	quantity	15806.8	3413	2752.1	9175.3	436.3
	proportion	-	21.8%	17.4%	58%	2.8%
sales income	quantity	16316.1	3631.5	2936.2	9279.8	498.6
	proportion	-	22.2%	18%	56.8%	3.1%
profit	quantity	939.6	323.6	174.3	391.2	50.5
	proportion	-	34.4%	18.6%	41.6%	5.4%

Table 3 The completion situation of economy index for main industry in 2005.

Unit: RMB billion

Index	Type	Above scale	Electricity	Machinery	Light industry	Petrol chemistry	Metallurgy	Automobile
Asset gross	quantity	15893.4	2421.28	2947.84	2397.32	1562.50	1743.80	1148.58
	proportion	-	15.2%	18.5%	15.1%	9.8%	11.0%	7.2%
Total production value	quantity	15806.8	3473.69	3134.83	2574.29	1892.66	1339.84	1043.06
	proportion	-	22.0%	19.8%	16.3%	12.0%	8.5%	6.6%
sales income	quantity	16316.1	3538.49	3158.24	2648.64	1890.73	1488.87	1186.81
	proportion	-	21.6%	19.3%	16.2%	11.6%	9.1%	7.3%
profit	quantity	939.6	54.36	226.04	129.87	67.26	178.33	99.58
	proportion	-	5.8%	24.1%	13.8%	7.2%	19.0%	10.6%

Index	Type	Textile	Electricity	Building materials	Colored	Medicine	Tobacco	Other
Asset gross	quantity	693.17	1161.75	320.61	152.03	304.18	421.42	618.95
	proportion	4.4%	7.3%	2.0%	1.0%	1.9%	2.7%	3.9%
Total production value	quantity	775.12	565.71	261.89	256.01	216.86	215.70	57.13
	proportion	4.9%	3.6%	1.7%	1.6%	1.4%	1.4%	0.4%
sales income	quantity	768.83	577.02	262.96	260.79	226.95	226.95	109.73
	proportion	4.7%	3.5%	1.6%	1.6%	1.4%	1.4%	0.7%
profit	quantity	31.79	41.13	9.90	8.64	71.10	71.10	5.70
	proportion	3.4%	4.4%	1.1%	0.9%	7.6%	7.6%	0.6%

(3) From the view of ownership systems: the industry overall production value realized by foreign-invested economy occupied 62.2%, the joint-stock system economy occupied 27.7%, the other ownership system economy occupied 10.1% (referring to table 4)

Table 4   The completion situation of economy main economic index on various ownership systems in 2005

Unit: RMB billion

Index	Type	Above scale	Foreign-invested	Joint-stock system	State-owned	Collective	Joint-stock cooperation	Other
Asset gross	quantity	15893.44	8398.48	5147.79	1808	229.57	136.32	173.28
	proportion	--	52.8%	32.4%	11.4%	1.4%	0.9%	1.1%
Total production value	quantity	15806.78	9828.19	4375.52	936.04	286.44	171.1	227.48
	proportion	--	62.2%	27.7%	5.9%	1.8%	1.1%	1.4%
sales income	quantity	16346.1	10112.68	4582.95	981.55	247.73	167.34	226.86
	proportion	--	61.9%	28.0%	6.0%	1.5%	1.0%	1.4%
profit	quantity	939.56	447.95	366.99	88.45	14.91	11.47	9.79
	proportion	--	47.7	39.1%	9.4%	1.6%	1.2%	1.0%

2. the new breakthrough obtained by technology creation .

(1) The overall situation of scientific and research input. In 2005,the scientific and research development of industry enterprise in this city input RMB 26.107 billion, a rise of 12.6%,than last year. the fund income used in research and experiment development activity reached to RMB12.083 billion, a rise of 30.2%, which occupied 45. 3% of research input. The strength of scientific and research input (The input of scientific and research development occupied the proportion of main operation income) reached to 1.6% .The production value of high-tech industry occupied industry proportion of 25.1% in the whole city. The possession rate of Independent intellectual property rights for high-tech industry was 27.5%, a rise of 0.6 percentage point, than the last year. At the end of 2005, the science and technology member in the industry enterprise was 75,700 thousand, the scientific and research authority was 479.The most capital for the input of scientific and research development invested by foreign and Hong Kong, Macao and Tai Wan was RMB17.533 billion, which occupied 65.7% of the whole city industry and exceed the proportion of 3.8 percentage point made up by the main operation income. The fund income used in research and experiment development activity was RMB9.094 billion, which occupied the input of scientific and research of 51.9%. The strength for the input of scientific and research development was 1.7%.

(2) In the aspect of implementing the strategy of developing the city through science, technology and education, boosting and integrating network software into the transferring platform in order to decline the implementing of the significant industry attack project on strategy of developing the city through science, technology and education such as fiber material; the whole set equipment of coal liquefaction, the practical input was RMB 470 million. The capital input of significant attack project on strategy of developing the city through science, technology and education was RMB 280 million resulting in forging and bringing a passel of creative group and forming a passel of Independent intellectual property rights in the aspect of core and key technology, among, applying the Chinese patent 94 projects (including to have authorized) and foreign patent 15 projects (including to have authorized),

obtaining 3 copyrights and 32 registered brand . The overall progress of project was excellent; having input gabbart between Wai Gao Qiaoaand Yang ShanGang shall be applied. the middle experiment equipment of Shenhua coal fluidified directly 6 ton / day have performed the long period experiment for the second time in Shanghai and realized successful operation 18 days of continual coal input. The ship that uses the production base of half com-bination crank put into production in Shanghai, formed the core manufacture technology of independent intellec-tual property rights and broke the monopolization of foreign enterprise. The 9 projects such as: super ship diesel engine was integrated into the second significant industry attack special project.

(3) In the aspect of forming independent intellectual property rights, the application patent of enterprise in the whole year was 22,000 thousand, which occupied the application quantity of 69% in the whole city and still exerted the main body function.134 patents new product was regarded as "the patent new product of Shanghai city in 2005"; the 29 enterprises was regarded as "the demonstration enterprise of independent intellectual property rights in Shanghai (cultivating enterprise)";93 projects were integrated into" the municipal absorption and creative plan", Panel display actuation chip included in 11 projects was integrated into the second "Promoting linkage special project of entire machine industry and the integrated circuit design industry" to speed up the construction of technology creative system that take enterprise as main body and take independent innovation as core. The whole city increased the 38 enterprise technology centers of municipal and provincial level; 1 technology center of state level; 2 the branch centers of state level; 84 enterprise technology centers of district level.

3. Industrial Investment Keeps Properly Increasing

Fig. 2 Comparison of Industrial Investment Increment between 2004 and 2005

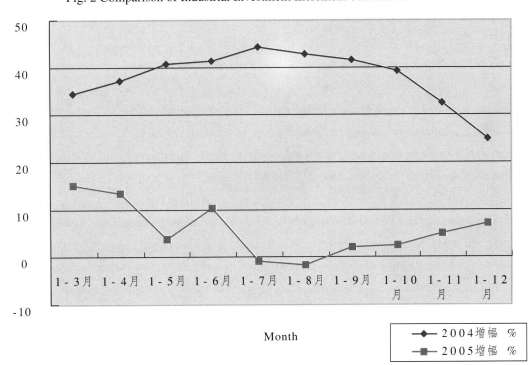

On the basis of high increment in 2004 (increased by 25.1% than 2003), the industrial investment in 2005 wholly was RMB107.48 billion, 7.3% higher than that of the same period last year. This was one year when investment increased gently since the implementation of the 10th Five– Year Plan. As viewed from investment of fixed asset of the city completely, about 15% increment maintained basically. Infrastructure Investment increased largely (more than 25%). The real estate development kept 10% above. The proportion of industrial investment in the city's investment was 30.3% (Fig. 2).

(1) As viewed from investment structure, investment on six main backbone industries was RMB 62.83 billion, accounting for 58.5% of the total investment on industries of the whole city. Among them, the investment increment on the equipment manufacturing industry was the highest one, with investment of RMB 14.28 billion, increased by 205%; on iron & steel industry, RMB 14 billion, increased by 52.4% than the same period last year; on automobile industry, RMB 8 billion, increased by 22.6% than the same period last year; on petroleum and chemical industry, RMB 11.14 billion, decreased by 41.9% than the same period last year; on electronic & information industry, RMB 14.24 billion, decreased by 31.8% than the same period last year; on biological pharmacy industry, RMB 1.8 billion, decreased by 7% than the same period last year (Fig. 3)

Flg.3 Investment Distribution of Six Backbone Industries

Electronics & information industry
Autombile manufacturing industry
Petroleum and chemical industry
Refined steel materials
Complete set equipment
Biological pharmacy industry
Other industries

(2) As viewed from the key investment points, in 2005 the investment was mainly for items of industry struc– ture adjustment and industry updating. The investment on equipment manufacturing industry was to improve the global equipment level and extreme manufacturing abilities of Shanghai electromechanical industry. The main invested items included the electrical port heavy equipment base with RMB 3.2 billion, the extension production project of large–scaled casting and forging member of Shanghai Heavy Machinery Plant, ship diesel generator of Ludong China Ship–Building (Group) Co. Ltd. with RMB 1.7 billion. The investment on petrochemical industry mainly included the world–leveled ethene project with capacity of million tons as well as the relevant items of isocyanate, phenol acetone and PVC. Investment on electronic and information industry was for the project of production line and post sealing of integrated circuit of 8 inches below 0.25 micron; Investment on iron and steel industry were for production line of wide & thick sheet which fills out the blank bracket, adjustment projects of production lines for stainless steel cold and hot rolling which substituted the imported products. Investment on automobile industry was for the reconstruction of the third Volswagon plant for new product development, the GM production extension project. The invested projects were featured with the extensive industries, high technology level and the heading level in the world nowadays.

(3) As viewed from the investment scale, in 2005 investment developed in scale drive. The key projects with total investment more than RMB 2 billion were 20. By the end of 2006, 6 of them will have been completed. They are: project of 5M wide and thick sheet invested RMB 6.8 billion, project of 1800 cold rolled steel strip invested

RMB 7.4 billion and the Phase II extension project of stainless steel production invested RMB 3.56 billion, Baoshan Iron & Steel Co. Ltd as well as the Phase II extension project of GM invested RMB 2.88 billion and the Shanghai Saike 900 thousand ton of ethene project invested RMB 22.4 billion.

(4) As viewed from ownership, in 2005 the state−owned investment kept the rising trend but the non−state−owned investment decreased slightly. According to the ownership classification, the state−owned investment was RMB 34.8 billion, accounting for one−third of the total industrial investment, increasing by 33.4% than that of the same period last year; the non−state−owned investment was RMB 73.2 billion, accounting for two−thirds of the total industrial investment, decreasing by 2% than that of the same period last year; the foreign investment decreased by 19.7% than that of the same period last year. But the folk investment increased rapidly, increasing by 38.9% than that of the same period last year

4. The industrial distribution structure was optimized increasingly.

Through several decades' distribution adjustment, the Shanghai industry has formed primarily the industrial distribution structure with characteristics of heading by the key industry base, working as main part by industries of counties and districts and playing the main carrier role by industrial parks and zones.

(1) Construct six backbone industries bases emphatically

In 2005, Shanghai focused on the construction of big industrial bases, establishing the main carriers of supporting the advanced manufacturing industry development. The six big industrial bases included the micro−electronics industry base, the automobile manufacturing industry base, the petrochemical industry base, refined steel material manufacturing base, the equipment manufacturing industry base and the ship manufacturing industry base.

(2) The district and county industries played an increasingly important role in the city economy

In 2005, the total industrial production from the nine districts of Pudong New Zone, Minhang, Baoshan, Jiading, Jinshan, Nanhui, Fengxian, Songjiang and Qingpu reached RMB 1342.83 billion, accounting for 85% of that of the whole city.

In the 19 districts and counties of the city, the total industrial production from Pudong New Zone was the highest. In 2005, its total industrial production reached RMB 376.314 billion, accounting for 23.8% of the total industrial production of the city. Both Minhang and Songjiang Districts were with the total industrial production over RMB 200 billion respectively; Baoshan and Jiading Districts over RMB 100 billion. Songjiang developed fast mostly. Its increment reached 36.7%; Minhang District, 25.7%.

(3) A new development was achieved on industries flowing into industrial parts and zones

In 2005, the total industrial production from the industrial zones at state level and at city level reached RMB 691.6 billion, increased by 43.8% than that in the same period last year. Shanghai Songjiang Export Processing Zone took the top rank in the other industrial development zones with its total industrial production of RMB 113. 218 billion and 52% increment. There were two development zones with the total industrial production exceeding RMB 100 billion; two zones with RMB 50 ~ 100 billion; six zones with RMB 20~50 billion. The industrial concentration in 2005 was increased to 53% from the previous 49% (including the six backbone industrial bases)

In 2005, the concentration of the heading industries in development zones improved further. The concentration of the heading industries in development zones above the city level reached more than 80%. In the development zones, the trend of centering several industries gatherings was formed such as three industries gatherings of electro—machinery, pharmacy & health care and foodstuff & beverage in Minhang Development Zone; industries gatherings of electronics and information, new materials, biological pharmacy and aerospace in Caohejing Development Zone; industries gathering of electronics and information, automobile and spare parts as well as household appliance in Jinqiao Development Zone; in Songjiang Industrial Zone, the electronics and information industry featured by computer making developed rapidly. The effect of industries gathering displayed further. The main business revenue of industries such as communication equipment, computer and other electronic equipment manufacturing reached RMB 315.854 billion, accounting for 89.3% of the same industries of the City; instruments and manufacturing industries for culture and office, 73.5%; manufacturing industry of transport equipment, manufacturing industry of electrical equipment and materials, manufacturing industries of raw chemical materials and products, their main business revenues all exceeded by 40% of the same industry of the city.

5. New patterns of industry opening to foreign countries were formed

In 2005, the export product values of industries in the city continued keeping the increment at high speed. The total value was RMB 499.089 billion, 29.2% higher than last year. This increment was largely higher than the total industrial production of the city.

In 2005, 10 industries export value exceeded RMB 10 billion. Among them, the general equipment manufacturing industry, transport equipment manufacturing industry, electric machinery and material manufacturing industry as well as computer and other electronic equipment manufacturing industry exceeded RMB 20 billion on export. Industries with export value increment by 50% included the timber processing and wooden, bamboo, rattan, palm and grass products industry, plastic product industry, general equipment manufacturing industry and special equipment manufacturing industry. Among them, the increment of special equipment manufacturing industry was the highest one, by 61.3%.

Songjiang District with Shanghai Songjiang Export Processing Zone and Pudong New Zone with Waigaoqiao Bonded Area and Jinqiao Export Processing Zone both are the important export base of the city. In 2005, their export values reached RMB 137.203 billion and RMB 120.975 billion respectively, totally accounting for 51.9% of export value of the city.

Investment economy from the foreign investor and Hongkong, Marco and Taiwan investors were the main power of export. In 2005, the above mentioned factors carried out RMB 441.529 billion on export, accounting for 88.6% of industry of the city.

(III) The national sequence order of shanghai industry

(1) The Shanghai industry has the drop in the national sequence order. Having played a crucial role in the nation, shanghai industry has the drop in the national sequence order, although most regional economy maintains the fast development in the 10th Five—Year Plan period. In 2005 the gross industrial production amount ranked the fifth in the nation. The first four are Guangdong, Jiangsu, Shandong, Zhejiang. The gross industrial production amount drops from 7.2% to 6% in the national proportion, the main business income, profit amount, and export delivery value accounts for 6.7%, 6.5%, and 10.4% respectively.

(2) The gross production amount of Guangdong province holds the first in the nation. The earlier starting of Guangdong economy and the large gap with other provinces and cities help to produce main business amount of RMB 3403,332 billion in 2005, up by 27.5% over 2004, and the profit amount of RMB 145,760 billion. In Guangdong industry development communication equipment, computer, and other electrical equipment manufac-

ture take the priority and other trades develop comprehensively. In 2005 the main business income of communication equipment, computer, and other electrical equipment manufacture of Guangdong province climbed to RMB 935,118 billion, taking up of 27.5% of provincial main business income, which is RMB 410,633 billion more than Jiangsu province ranking the second, and RMB 581,269 billion more than Shanghai.

(3) Jiangsu province keeps a rising development trend in the 10th Five-Year Plan period. In 2005 the completed main business income accounts for RMB 3212,952 billion, up by 28.8% over last year and the produced profit accounts for RMB 138,654 billion. Jiangsu province possesses most trades with large scale and there are seven industrial trades whose main business incomes surpass RMB 100 billion such as textile industry, chemistry raw material and chemical product manufacturing industry, ferrous metal smelting and rolling processing industry, general purpose equipment manufacturing industry, electrical machinery and equipment manufacturing industry, transportation equipment manufacturing industry, communication equipment, computer and other electronic equipment manufacturing industry whose rising development trend driven the development of the provincial economy. In shanghai there are four industrial enterprises whose main business incomes surpass RMB 100 billion, among which only communication equipment, computer and other electronic equipment manufacturing industry surpass RMB 300 billion, and ferrous metal smelting and rolling processing industry, transportation equipment manufacturing industry, and general purpose equipment manufacturing industry are less than RMB 150 billion in average in main business amount.

(4) Shandong province keeps a rapid development speed in the 10th Five-Year Plan period. In 2005 the completed main business income accounts for RMB 2991,084 billion, up by 43% over last year and the produced profit accounts for RMB 213.815 billion. Shandong province possesses the advantage of developed mining industry, crude oil production resource which get more profits when international crude oil price is rising, and the lost advantageous traditional industries in shanghai (as textile industry) developed rapidly in Shandong. In 2005 the efficiency of the most industrial trades is increased and the advantage of the foundational industry is prominent. Among 39 industrial trades 38 trades raised the profit amount than last year, of which there are 6 trades whose profit amount is above RMB 10 billion and the increasing extent is high: petroleum and natural gas mining industry, textile industry, chemistry raw material and chemical product manufacturing industry, agricultural & sideline products processing industry, coal mining and washing out industry, and non-metallic mineral product industry increase to76.3%, 76.2%, 68.5%, 67.8%, 47.8%, and 40.7% respectively; there are seven industries whose profits range RMB 5-10 billion.

(5) Zhejiang industry balanceable development In 2005 the main business income Zhejiang province completed accounts for RMB 2170.247 billion, a rise of 24.7%, with the produced profit of RMB 107.283 billion. Zhejiang was taken the private enterprise as the main body, the main business income of private industrial enterprise in Zhejiang occupied the proportion of above scale industrial enterprise reached to34.6% ,the contribution rate for industrial tax,the growth of profit was 43.7% 49.4%, hauling the tax and profit raised 5.9 and 5.7 percentage point respectively. Industry balanceable development was the most characteristic of Zhejiang industry. Not having the super scale industry and the change insinuation of unit industry can not produce influence for the entire industry, and the industry operation achievement of 70% industry were better than the same line in all-around country to make the industry economy keep excellent development trend for the provincial industry.

(6) The comparison of 5 cities and provinces economy development .From the view of development aftereffect,

in the near tow years, the fixed asset investment of Shanghai industry was far inferior to other 4 municipals and provincials, One of the reason for Shanghai industry production rise slackened was that the investment lowered the industry hauling function and influence the industry development aftereffect in the future directly .in 2005,the investment of industry fixed asset in this city was RMB107.476 billion, a rise of 7.3%,than last year and occupied the proportion of industry fixed asset investment in the whole society that returned 2.2 percentage point than last year. among, the investment of 6 key development industry was RMB 62.837 billion,only a rise of 1.4%.(referring to table 5).

Table 5   The comparison of fixed asset investment amount in near two years five provinces and cities industry.

Unit: RMB billion

Province and city	2004 year	Increment (%)	2005 year	Increment (%)
Shanghai	1001.02	25.1	1074.76	7.3
Shandong	2816.00	34.3	4007.02	42.3
Jiangsu	2101.92	26.2	2765.02	31.6
Zhejiang	2704.07	35.3	2942.05	22.4
Guangdong	1639.02	31.4	2722.82	32.1

(In the above table, the data caliber of Shanghai, Shandong, Jiangsu and Guangdong province exceed the town in 2004;the Zhejiang, Guangdong province in 2005 exceed the limited quantity)

(IV). The influence of energy supply on industry development

In 10th Five-Year Plan, the supply and the price variation of electricity, coal, and petroleum has produced a big influence on city's industry production and economical movement.

(1) Electricity. In 10th Five-Year Plan, because national economy development speed was enhanced, electricity and coal supply strains in many places, furthermore, the shortage of coal supply intensifies the strain of electricity supply. The limited electricity generation capacity and the increased difficulty in purchasing electricity from outside also caused the shortage of electricity supply, meanwhile years of unceasing the highest electricity load in summer high-temperature period produced a bad effect on industry production. In order to solve the shortage of electricity supply in summer high-temperature period the related offices and companies in city should try to deal with not only to guarantee the normal supply of electricity and normal production of industrial enterprises but also to prevent the temporary cut off or limit electricity. Enterprises should speed up production ahead in the first and second quarter and elaborately arrange electricity production and priority plan in summer high-temperature period ahead to reduce the influence of shortage of electricity supply on city industrial production to the lowest.

(2) Coal. In the 10th Five-Year Plan electricity and coal supply strained in the city and coal storage amount drops in large scale which are frequently urgent. So the related offices as well as big-coal-consuming party altogether go to purchase coal actively in coal production site to guarantee the normal coal consumption of industrial enterprises in city. But the big increase of coal price in the 10th Five-Year Plan period also increase the production cost of industrial enterprises.

(3) Cause. In the 10th Five-Year Plan period the variation of Middle-East situation caused the constant

rising of crude oil price in international market, furthermore, influenced industrial enterprises production largely. Petrochemical and refined chemical manufactures whose basic material was crude oil were highlighted to develop inferior to electrical information products in total amount. The products of petrochemical and refined chemical manufactures were divided into superior, middle, and inferior in which crude oil directly influenced superior products and indirectly influenced middle, and inferior products. There are only two companies——petrochemical Company and Gaohua Company which produced superior products. In 2005, annual crude oil production amount climbed to 19.9592 million tons and of all used crude above oil 95% depends on export, however the price of the finished oil is controlled by the state. The big increase of crude oil price in international market and the serious scissors gap between the prices of international crude oil and finished oil caused the two companies in recent years to be in the state of serious deficit. The lower products——non-production chemistry products, because of sharp price competition, faced the pressure of chemical material price rising and had to digest in themselves, unfortunately part of enterprises or products (such as washing powder and other daily necessities) had stopped production or reduce production because of large deficit amount. The price of the Middle products——chemical material as the beneficiary of the price rising of crude oil, when crude oil price raises, rises simultaneously. And the price rising extent is above crude oil price rising extent, so once was the main benefit-earning party prior crude oil price rising in chemical industry. But in the second half year of 2004, the cutting off or reducing production of lower products reduce the need of chemical material, meanwhile much more chemical material factories newly opened at home, sharp market competition, and the slower price rising of chemical material also make production enterprises profit drop.

(4) Natural gas. As a new type energy, except Donghai Natural gas, in the 10th Five-Year Plan period, natural gas in the strategy of transporting the natural gas from the West to the East began to be provided. But comparing with the anticipated supply amount of the natural gas in the strategy of transporting the natural gas from the West to the East, the actual acquired amount is far less than planned supply amount, therefore it took a bad effect on city industrial production. The insufficient supply amount was only supplied for the normal living of residents, so forced some industrial enterprises with natural gas being the main energy to stop production.

II. Analysis on 2006 Shanghai industry development environment

1. World Economy Trend

The international organization is of limit optimism on 2006 global economy. In 2006, the world economy will move forward on stable track. The world economy increment will continue the track of 2005 and maintain equally with that in 2005, keeping the moderate increment speed. Economy in counties with high income will keep the stable operation because of the stable increment of USA, Europe and Japan. The US economy is still the main power of the world economy increment. Economy increment of most developing countries will be higher than the average lever of the world. The affect on the world economy increment from some developing countries such as China, India and others will be more important increasingly. The world trade in 2006 will continue actively. The increment of the world trade will continue keeping at the higher increment level.

In 2006, the uncertain factors which threaten the world economy increment include mainly the global financial unbalance, the continuing large rising of petroleum price, bird flu infecting human being as well as the possible abrupt drop of house price caused by the over-heated real estate market of not expensive scheduled house. In

2006, the global revenue and expenditure face the unbalance. The often account trade deficit and the rapid rising net debt of the USA will result in the disaster depreciation of US dollar. The world economy will be impacted largely by side effect. Lots of developing countries will face the difficulty in the pressure of monetary appreciation and the rising of foreign currency reserve. In short period, the petroleum supply in the world market will still be intension. Inflation rate in the world in 2006 will increase slightly. But, due to the limit transfer of energy price rising to the general price, the inflation rate is expected to be lower and stable. However, should the energy price keep at high level or continue rising, the pressure of the rising of inflation rate will be large. Trade protectionism and trade friction will be on stage. The non−tariff barrier to trade in the world will occur. This, in certain of extent, will counterweight the power caused by tariff exemption for encouraging the increment of the world trade.

2. Domestic policy environment

In 2006, china economy will continue the good trend of keeping stable and fast growth. Stability is the basic principle of macro economic policy in 2006. The State will continue reinforcing and improving the macro adjust−ment and control, keep the continuity and stability of the macro economic policy; continue implementing the stable and sound financial policy and monetary policy. Simultaneously, the micro adjustment shall be performed to the newly occurred issues. Regarding economic development, the State will focus on adjusting the economic structure, varying the economic growth manner, improving the economic benefits and ensure the suitable growth rate of the economy, realizing development fast and soundly.

Enlarging the domestic demands is the long−term strategy and the basic standing point of economic develop−ment of our country. In 2006, this point will be put more important position. In accordance with requirements of building the new socialism countryside, the State will be devoted on effectively initiating the countryside market and increasing the resident consumption especially the farmer consumption. This will be the key point of enlarging the consumption demands, changing the investment direction, realizing the significant transferring from urban construction mainly to countryside construction more.

In 2006, land and credit management of macro adjustment shall be continued controlling well to prevent the investment inflation from rebounding, and push the adjustment on some over−production industry. Item and com−pany not complying with industry policy and market access condition as well as required to wash out by the State, the State further emphasizes the loan and land will not be provided, and the relevant organization of environment protection and safety supervision shall not issue the relevant formalities.

To carry out the State guideline of medium−long term science and technology development plan and build the innovated country, the State will reinforce the support intensity on initiative innovation in 2006. The financial expenditure on science and technology shall be increased by 19.2% than last year. This increment obviously is higher than financial income and expenditure. Simultaneously, through favorable tax policies such as tax deduction, exemption and speeding up depreciation as well as government purchase, establish the environment of encourag−ing innovation, push the enterprise to be the main body of innovation and promote the progress of science and technology.

Reforms of the state−owned enterprises, the stock system of commercial banks and the separation of stock and right are the main tasks. The reform of product prices of resources such as petroleum and natural gas will be written on the agenda. To result in the obvious achievement of saving energy resources, the high−energy consump−tion industries and enterprises such as iron & steel, nonferrous, electric power and building materials shall be forced according to laws to wash out the behindhand technologies, workmanship and products. Environment protection shall be paid more attention and introduced to exam and inspect the local government and leaders. And the examination and inspection results will be publicized periodically.

3. Development environment of Shanghai itself

2006 is the first year of implementing the 11th Five-Year Plan. Shanghai faces the new development environment of how to reinforce the international competition force, follow the innovation-driving track, transfer the growth manner and growth power.

(1) The enterprise initiative innovation steps in a new stage. Shanghai, according to the relevant policies of the State and combining the Shanghai actual situation, carries out the detailed rules of relevant policies, focuses on key sectors, break through the key bottleneck, speed up carrying out the scientific development concept and implement strongly the strategy of science and education prospering the city, and form the technical innovation system of enterprise as main body, market as orientation, and combination of production, learning and studying, improve the encouraging system of enterprise innovation and guide Shanghai t follow the initiative innovation track.

(2) Construction of new suburb and new countryside of Shanghai will be fully pushed forward. The building of new modernization suburb with the characteristics of international metropolis is the key task of Shanghai development in the 11th Five-Year Plan. In 2006, Shanghai will focus on agriculture modernization, speed up the construction of modern suburb and township, and fully push forward the countryside comprehensive reform. Suburb industrial development, planning, population and environment will be completely paid more attention.

(3) Supply and safety of energy resource will be paid more attention unprecedented. Energy and environment protection are the important targets listed in the 11th Five-Year Plan. Shanghai faces the hard task of decreasing the energy consumption of unit GDP by 20%. Regarding the energy saving, compared with the developed country, Shanghai has a long way to go but also is with large potential. This year, much stronger measures will be taken. Development and saving will be important simultaneously and saving shall be in priority in order to ensure the energy supply and energy safety.

(4) Reform and opening-up face new opportunity and environment. Trial of comprehensive complement reform of Pudong New Zone is one good development opportunity entrusted by the central government. In 2006, Shanghai will utilize the effect of Pudong reform to realize the actual breakthrough on linkage between Pudong and Puxi. In 2006, Shanghai also will finish basically the goal and task of three-year reform of holding company, completely furnish the reform of separation of stock and right of the state-owned listed holding company. The reforms of stated-owned asset and enterprises will enjoy the better system environment and development room. 2006 is the last year of transition period after China's access to WTO. Shanghai will utilize the advanced advantage on opening of service trade to attract more multi-national companies in fields of finance, trade and manufacturing to establish their region headquarter, operation center and study development center in Shanghai

(5) Speed up developing modern service industry and advanced manufacturing industry. In 2006, Shanghai will increasingly develop work concept, innovate work method and strongly develop the intensity of modern service industry; take the gathering area of modern service industries as the breakthrough, strongly develop financial industry, logistic industry, cultural innovation industry and productive service industry so as to harvest the new achievement on industrial structure while service economy is mainly formed and realize the new breakthrough.

(6) A group of important infrastructure and key developing items specified in the 11th Five-Year Plan move

into investment and construction period. In 2006, the world's fair project will be fully initiated. The track transport will step into the peak construction period. The largely invested projects such as airport reconstruction and extension as well as the sequent works of Yangshan Harbor will be commenced successfully. The industrial investment in 2006 will keep proper growth. The increment will be equal to that last year. The petroleum and chemical projects as well as the integrated circuit enterprises will initiate a second investment and production extension. More investment will be guided to the new-energy automobile manufacturing project and the manufacturing industry of innovative manufacturing equipment of important domestic equipment which have obvious driving and support function on industrial updating and science & education prospering the city.

III. The highlight of development policies of Shanghai industry in 2006

1. Strengthen the economic performance adjustment earnestly.

Perfect the work focuses————"forecast, early-warning, pre-arranged planning and anticipating control" and make sure the whole year's two "two double-figure increases". The electronic, mechanical, light-industrial, petrol-chemical, metallurgical and automobile industries with the annual output of RMB 100 billion shall be oriented as the key industries; the 20 enterprises with various forms of ownership, such as Semiconductor Manufacturing International Corporation (SMIC), BYD Electronics, Shanghai Zhenhua Port Machinery Co., Ltd. (ZPMC), Guangdian Power NEC, Kaiquan Pump Industry MF. Co., Ltd. Shall be oriented as the key enterprises; 21 kinds of products, such as LCD, panel TV, integrated circuit, car, air-conditioner compressor, finished steel, product oil, ethane, tire cover, machine tool, etc., shall be oriented as the key products; and 4 areas, such as Songjiang, Minxing, Pudong and Jiading, shall be oriented as the key areas, and also the dynamic tracking shall be further enhanced. The forecast shall be detailed, thus to further improve the monthly forecasting network of industrial production and the quarterly forecasting network of industrial effectiveness, track the promulgation of national crucial policies, the great international and domestic affairs and hot problems, and further satisfy the 3 monitoring networks on the economic performance analysis, the export and import price and market price of key products and the industry safety forecast. Make sure stable supply of important energies and raw materials in Shanghai, such as coal, electricity, gas, etc., and make sure above 14 days of coal and above 7 days of product oil on stock, to realize the stable resource supply in emergency. Promote the strategic cooperation between Shanghai City and Shen Hua Group Co, Ltd. and make efforts to quicken the establishment of the coal storage base in Shanghai, thus to relieve Shanghai's shortage of the coal resource ultimately.

2. Make efforts to buildup innovation ability of the enterprise.

Aiming at "concentrating on the enterprise's main subject and enhancing the innovation ability", take effective measures to strive for obvious improvement of all enterprises' innovation abilities of Shanghai City in 3-5 years. Firstly, implement self-innovation on key installations. Actively carry out Opinions on accelerating to invigorate the equipment manufacturing industry of the State Council, work out the Detailed rules on accelerating innovation of key installations of Shanghai. The relative departments shall establish the coordination mechanism, based on the economic regulations and market rules, through encouragement to the users and manufactories, set up the risk bearing mechanism, and break through the achievement on the first set of key technology installations, realizing the coordination between the key project and the key technology installation. Secondly, promote the strategic alliance among the production, study and research systems. The enterprise shall develop its leading function in cooperation on production, study and research systems, and in the key industrialized project, the enterprise shall be the presenter of the technical innovative project, to push forward the industrialization of innovation projects and the commercialization of innovation achievements. The close cooperation among those systems shall be encouraged, thus to establish innovative integrated organizations of all forms, the R&D organization shall be the main power to study the project and tackle the technology. It's required to combine and build the information connection platform among these systems, to strengthen coordination mechanism and promote integration on these systems. Thirdly, improve input on the enterprise innovation. It's necessary to help the enterprise implement all policies concerning the enterprise innovation encouraged by the state and Shanghai, to support the enterprise to increase R&D input, and to carry the national key industrialized technology project. It's required to increase the government's support to enterprise innovation, to develop the fiscal capital's encouraging function and enlarging function to enterprise innovation, and to encourage the conditional enterprise to buy the advanced technology, R&D equipment and testing apparatus. It's required to encourage the enterprise to improve its financing ability, to use fund of the capital market, and to continuously extend the financing channel. Fourthly, push the industrial area to become the carrier of enterprise innovation. Some experiment zones shall be expanded in Shanghai, to build the technical service platform for industry, improve the industry technical information system, and construct an opening system served for the enterprise innovation. The advanced manufacturing commonness and public technical platforms, such as the micro−electron, system software, modern Chinese traditional medicine, bio−engineering, nanometer technology, telecommunication technology, new material, etc., shall be stressfully built up. Experiment units shall be implemented in well−conditioned industrial zones, such as Caohejing Hi−tech Park, Shanghai Chemical and Industrial Zone, International Automobile City, Lingang Industrial Park, Xinzhuang Industrial Zone, etc. Fifthly, introduce and cultivate technical innovative elites. Promote the "ten thousand, thousand, hundred and ten " elites development plan of the state−owned enterprise, emphatically cultivate and attract the leader of the technical innovation, pace−setters in scientific research, scientific and technological professional and technical worker. Encourage the conditional enterprise to arrange Chief Technology Officer to increase technical staff's position in the enterprise's leadership. Make full use of the special technical person and technical worker's active use in enterprise innovation.

3. Fully promote the construction of industry base.

In 2006, the key construction projects are 6 key projects totaled RMB 10 billion, 20 key industry upgrading projects totaled above RMB 2 billion, 10 strategic upgrading projects of equipment manufacturing industry and 10 modern logistic projects, with total investment capital of about RMB 150 billion. After completion, the newly added sales income shall be estimated at about RMB 200 billion and above one third of the projects shall be finished and put into production in 2006. The main projects are listed as the following, BAOSTEEL Automobile Plate Production line of the Silicon Steel, Luojing COREX, and NO. 1 STEEL Stainless Steel Cold−rolled project, Bayer Polycarbonate, United Carbimide and Huasheng Chemical and Industrial Caustic Soda & Chlorethene projects of the Chemical and Industrial Zone, the second period of generation 5 TFT project of Shangguangdian Power NEC, SMIC Shenya Micron Integrated Circuit project, Shanghai Automobile Engineering Research Institute, Shanghai Electron Lingang Equipment Base, etc. Firstly, perfect the investment project base. Based on "constructing a number of projects, putting into production with a number of projects, and storing a number of projects", enrich and perfect the storage of investing construction projects, and according to the project recording and ratification man−

agement method, improve the e-network of storage and make out the investment analysis, project land-using analysis, etc., an work out the three-year rolling plan from2006-2008. It's necessary to build up the coordination mechanism of key projects, strengthen connection among the related government departments, build up the green channel on key projects, quicken the project construction speed, and keep the future growth of Shanghai industry. Work out the management method on promoting Shanghai key investment projects, form the criteria for the requirement, procedure, support policy, land policy and relative services listed in the key project and "four preferences" shall be fulfilled to the key project, via, preferably arranging into Shanghai key projects, preferably arranging into key coordination, preferably ensuring land supply and preferably supplying capital support. Aiming at the shortage of land resource in Shanghai and the realization of self-innovation, with the support of government preferential policies (such as information, etc.), it shall be to encourage the enterprise to conduct technical innovation and technical adoption, optimize the industry structure, enhance the enterprise competitiveness, advance the industry upgrading and step forward to sustainable development. Fourthly, develop new management on the industrial and commercial industry investment. It's necessary to perfect the recording and ratification management of investment projects of Shanghai industrial and commercial enterprises, work out the detailed implementation rules, and start to build the recording and ratification platform on net for the industrial and commercial investment projects. Simplify the procedure and shorten the preparatory work time for the project. Increase the training work at the district, county and group corporation and straighten out the management network.

4. Optimize the policy environment of industry development.

Firstly, carry out related policies supporting the industry development earnestly. At the beginning of this year, the state promulgated 60 policies aiming at strengthening self-innovation, and opinions concerning invigorating the equipment manufacturing industry (Guofa [2006] No.8), and Shanghai worked out the implementation advices on carrying out supporting policies concerning the national compendium of the medium- and long-term scientific development. The relative departments of Shanghai shall work together to carry out supporting polices to the enterprises, to reduce the cost and risk of enterprise self-innovation. Grasp the chance of supporting experiments on Pudong integrated reform, actively strive for the first-try of key national policies in Pudong and develop the anticipatory effectiveness. Secondly, promulgate the new guide on industrial and technical innovation. Related departments shall work out and issue the new guide on industrial and technical innovation, specify key fields of innovation at all industries, compile the technology and product guide of innovation encouraged by Shanghai, set up the specific items, such as introduction, adoption and innovation, the innovative system of enterprise technology, self-innovation of key installations, demonstrating enterprise of the intellectual property, new patented product, etc., lead and organize the enterprise to concentrate on key projects, and improve the technical grade of industry. Based on the "11th Five-Year" Plan and the Action Plan on Preferentially Developing the Advanced Manufacturing, present the industry investment guide and support policies, compile the Guide on Industry Investment in Shanghai, and guide the social capital investment. Thirdly, formulate the joined force on promoting industry development. As the supervising department, the economic and trade commission shall strengthen work, such as guiding the industry, perfecting innovation environment, constructing the service platform, and supplying policy supports; as to the central enterprise, support its settlement in Shanghai, and strive for more important projects with high self-innovation and national strategy; as to the city-owned group, promote the linkage between it and the reform of state-owned enterprise in industry development and technical innovation; and as to the private enterprise and the hi-tech enterprise originated by the returnee elites, optimize the environment, supply the service platform and help them be out of problems in development. As to the medium- and small- sized enterprises, grasp the detailed advance based on the work net at the district and county levels and emphatically coordinate the common and bottleneck problems. At the same time, develop the function of the study institute, R&D organization, industry association and agency in innovation. Study ways, such as the government purchasing the service, develop the industry association's function, and support the industry association to carry research, brand promotion, information service, etc. based on its ability and industry characteristics.

5. Promote the intensive development of energy and resource.

In energy saving, it's necessary to grasp the key energy consuming unit, key energy-consuming equipment and unit loss of key products, and improve the management skill of energy. Encourage the enterprise to adopt technical innovation to quicken reconstruction of energy-saving and enhance the working efficiency. Firstly, promote a number of key energy-saving projects and key items. The following key energy-saving projects shall be implemented, such as the power saving on industrial electrical equipment, optimization of the energy system, energy saving on the surplus heat and pressure use, coal saving of the industrial coal-fired boiler and furnace, energy saving of construction, power saving of the air conditioner and household appliance, green lighting, distributed power supply, energy saving of the government departments, municipal transportation saving, replacing petroleum, etc. Secondly, actively enhance the demonstrating experiment work of the solar energy and other new energy sources and fine energy sources use. Practice the demonstrating experiment unit of solar energy and green lighting, through the government purchase or support, and increase the extension of new energy source and energy saving product. In 2006, projects of energy saving sources, such as the solar energy, green lighting demonstration, etc., shall be constructed, in accordance with the construction projects, such as Waigaoqiao, Wuqiao grain warehouse, Chuangyi zone of No. 8, Luwan district, reconstruction of the road lamp system at Sichuangbeilu road of Hongkou Zone, standardized vegetable market, modern service integrated zone, Lingang Xincheng, etc. Thirdly, build up the innovation system of social service enhancing the energy saving. Strengthen the ability construction of transmitting organization on energy efficiency, gradually build up the information network of energy efficiency management covering the key power using units and key buildings, issue the energy use bulletin, and provide information, consultation and training on energy saving. Promote the perfect work of EMC. At the same time, take the opportunity of the energy saving propagating week, strengthen the training force on the propagation of energy saving and integrated using, guide all society to take part in the construction of the energy saving and environmental city, and form the better social prevailing custom that the whole society participate the energy saving. In promoting the construction of recycling economy, firstly, carry out the construction of demonstrating industrial park of recycling economy. Promote the enterprise to spread the experiment construction of cleaner production, and in 2006 the focus is to do well the cleaner production in electro-plate industry. At the same time, combining "the third round of three-year environment protecting plan", implement recycling economic experiments at conditional industrial zone, such as Xinzhuang, Baoshan, etc. Secondly, fully develop the energy source integrated using. Strengthen the reclaim utilization rate of the renewable and recyclable resources, such as the waste paper, waste glass, waste metal, waste appliance, etc. In 2006, the construction of Shanghai electronic waste dealing center shall be focused to actively explore the way on composing Shanghai electronic waste dealing framework. Emphasize the integrated use on high-calcium fly ash, devulcanized ash of the power plant, etc. Thirdly, vigorously advocate green consumption.

Guide and expand simple package, support the industry association to compile and implement the industry self-regulation on suggested goods package, and in 2006, the health care product, cosmetics and food industries shall be oriented to control excessive package of goods.